Love is
a time of enchantment:
in it all days are fair and all fields
green. Youth is blest by it,
old age made benign:
the eyes of love see
roses blooming in December,
and sunshine through rain. Verily
is the time of true-love
a time of enchantment — and
Oh! how eager is woman
to be bewitched!

A QUESTION OF LOVE

Desperate for her independence, Pippa flies to Minorca as secretary to Gene Watson, an American film star writing his explosive reminiscences of Hollywood. She is flattered by the attentions of the wealthy Spaniard Juan y Correa, but does he really love her? Why is he so suspicious? Pippa does not realise the real danger she is in until it is almost too late.

BRIDGET THORN

A QUESTION OF LOVE

Complete and Unabridged

ULVERSCROFT
Leicester

First published in Great Britain in 1984 by
Robert Hale Limited
London

First Large Print Edition
published March 1992

British Library CIP Data

Thorn, Bridget
    A question of love.—Large print ed.—
Ulverscroft large print series: romance
I. Title
823.914 [F]

ISBN 0–7089–2616–9

Published by
F. A. Thorpe (Publishing) Ltd.
Anstey, Leicestershire

Set by Words & Graphics Ltd.
Anstey, Leicestershire
Printed and bound in Great Britain by
T. J. Press (Padstow) Ltd., Padstow, Cornwall

1

PIPPA glanced at her watch and frowned. She was half an hour early for her interview. Then the first heavy drops of rain began to fall and she wished yet again that she had thought to bring an umbrella. She looked nervously at the gorgeously attired doormen at the imposing entrance to the hotel and then suddenly made up her mind. Surely it would be possible for her to wait inside until it was time for her to meet her prospective employer.

Bracing herself she crossed the forecourt and smiled in relief as one of the doormen, looking more like a retired admiral than a flunkey, opened the door and ushered her through. Somehow she had expected these English hotels to be like fortresses, admitting only the very wealthy or the famous with such ease.

With growing confidence she approached the man seated behind an impressive reception desk.

"I have an appointment with Mr Watson at eleven. Is there some place I can wait, please?"

"Coffee lounge, ma'am, first floor. Turn right at the top of those stairs," he added, and Pippa reminded herself that the English used the term ground floor for the first one. She grinned as she turned away. It was the first time she had been called ma'am, and somehow the term did not suit her petite figure. There was a huge mirror on the half landing and she paused momentarily, her deep brown eyes glinting in amusement as she silently addressed herself as "Madam Dawson". Then she stepped closer to the mirror to pat into place a stray curl, and scrutinize her appearance carefully.

She nodded at length, satisfied. Her discreet dark green skirt and crisp white shirt, topped with a full length dark green coat, looked eminently suitable for the applicant for a confidential secretary's job. The plain black shoes and shoulder bag looked dull, but she had an instinct that anything more frivolous would mitigate against her chances of getting this job. And it was suddenly crucially important that she was accepted.

She frowned slightly and stepped back from the mirror, and gasped as she collided with a man running lightly up the stairs.

"Oh, I — I beg your pardon!" she exclaimed, hastily disentangling herself from the arm which he had instinctively thrown round her to prevent her from falling.

She glanced up at him. He was tall, at least six foot, and had wide, powerful looking shoulders encased in a dark, beautifully cut jacket of fine, expensive tweed. He wore a white silk polo necked sweater and fawn cord pants, but it was his face that held Pippa's gaze.

He was dark, almost swarthy. His hair was smooth and black, slightly long but well cut and immaculate. His eyes were narrowed as he looked down at Pippa, and were of a startlingly bright blue. A thin face, with high cheekbones and a narrow, almost delicately moulded nose. His lips, parted now to reveal even white teeth, were thin but well shaped. She judged him to be about thirty.

"Madam can be forgiven for having

become lost in the contemplation of such beauty," he said smoothly, and with a slight bow stepped round her and continued up the stairs, running swiftly and easily and disappearing before Pippa's swift flush had risen from her neck to her cheeks.

She swallowed, then giggled. She had been called madam twice within a few minutes. Yet he must have considered her vain to stand there apparently admiring her reflection, and for some reason that hurt, for she was not conceited about her looks.

She did herself an injustice when she thought of herself as ordinary. Small and neat, her body was nonetheless shapely, slim and yet curvaceous at the right places. Her hair which she wore cut short was naturally curly. It was very dark but had a faintly auburn glow in certain lights. Big dark brown eyes gazed from beneath thick eyebrows which Pippa deplored, but which added considerably to the charm of her heart-shaped face. She had a small straight nose and full, generous lips which were usually curved in amusement, for Pippa enjoyed life and often found both herself and other people slightly ridiculous.

Then she shrugged and continued up the stairs. She had just given her order for coffee when a voice behind her spoke.

"Pippa! Have you seen him yet?"

She went rigid before slowly turning to face the young man who had spoken.

"Frank! How did you know where I was?" she demanded.

He hooked out a chair with his toe and sat facing her.

"Dolores told me when I phoned the flat. Look, you can't just run away to the other side of the world because we had a row. Have you seen this fellow yet?"

"Not yet, and Minorca is not exactly the other side of the world," she pointed out calmly.

"It will be when I'm back in California," he said angrily. "A bourbon for me," he added as the waiter deposited the tray of coffee on the table.

"I'm sorry, sir, the bar is not open," the waiter replied. "Will you have coffee?"

Frank bit back his remark and nodded. "These stupid rules about when you

5

can drink!" he muttered as the man went away.

"It's rather early in the day to be swigging bourbon!" Pippa replied sharply. "Frank, we discussed this last night. I'm not coming straight home. I'm not ready to marry you yet."

"But why, it's been understood for years!"

"It may have been what our fathers wanted, since they're cousins and partners and that would be a way of ensuring that the business isn't split," she said slowly, "but I never agreed."

"But you came to England to see me," he pointed out triumphantly.

"I came for a long vacation after finishing college," she said quickly. "Dolores invited me, and as we'd been pen pals for years and never met it seemed a good opportunity. It was nice that you were still here doing your course, but I didn't come only to see you."

"But why this sudden urge to get a job?"

"I've never had one except casual jobs during the vacations, and most of those Dad arranged with his friends. I want to

6

prove that I can get and hold down a job on my own."

She watched him as he sat back, waiting as the new tray of coffee was placed before him, then she leant over and poured for them both. Muttering his thanks Frank lifted his cup and sat with it warming his hands. His fair hair hung over one eye, and his face was slightly flushed. He was goodlooking in a sporty, healthy way, and his long muscular legs in his normal jeans were those of an athlete.

Why could she not accept his love? Pippa knew that many of her college friends had envied her his devotion, his constant attention and willingness to escort her wherever she wished to go, but she felt stifled by it. She had known him all her life and the two families had often spent vacations together. Frank, two years older than she, had taught her to swim and to ski, to dance and drive, and had tried to teach her to love him. In this last he had failed although it had only been when he had left California to take a college course in London that she had realised it.

Suddenly free to accept invitations from other men, she had realised with a shock that Frank meant little more to her than any of the casual dates who took her out. His kisses meant no more to her than those of anyone else, and she had developed a reluctance to marry without some greater feeling than that.

"You could get a job in the States for a while," he said suddenly. "I wouldn't wish to hurry you, darling. I want to get started in the business before we get married."

"I've told you I can't marry you, Frank," she said gently. "It's not only wanting a job. That's separate. First, I don't love you as I'd want to love the man I married, and secondly, if I were at home, even if I went to Boston or Washington or New York, I'd still have Dad looking over my shoulder to make sure I was doing nothing wrong, and ready to leap in and protect me or rescue me if there was the slightest sign of any problem. I want to prove that I can cope on my own and I'd never do that in the States."

"But Minorca!" he exclaimed. "At

least you could stay in England."

"It's not so easy to get a job here," she pointed out, growing impatient. "Besides, this one looks interesting although I haven't got it yet."

They argued for a while and then Pippa gasped as she saw the time.

"Heavens, it's a minute to eleven! It won't make a good impression if I'm late. Sorry, Frank, I must run. I'll phone this evening, I promise."

She hurried out of the coffee lounge and up another flight of stairs. The suite of rooms she was looking for was down the corridor to the right and she hurried anxiously along, scanning the numbers on the doors. She had almost reached the right one when Frank caught up with her and seized her arm.

"Pippa! You can't do this! What will everyone say at home? They expected us to announce our engagement as soon as we got back. I'll not let you make a fool of me. It's been accepted for years that you're mine!"

"I belong to no-one but myself!" Pippa said, dangerously quiet. She rarely lost her temper but when she did it resembled, her mother had once laughingly said, a sudden unheralded explosion. There were a few moments of deathly calm and then the crack of thunder and lightning which annihilated everything in its way.

"We need not get married straight away," Frank said desperately, "but I won't permit you to marry anyone else!"

"You won't permit me? Just who do you think you are, Frank? You've no claim on me, no rights, and I shall marry just whoever I choose! If I want to marry a senile old man for his money there's nothing you or anyone else can do to stop me! I'm going my own way from now on and whatever you may have thought I made you no promises! I will not go home with you! Now go away!"

Breathing deeply she swung round and raised her hand to hammer on the door of the suite behind her, and once more collided with the man she had met on the stairs. Too furious to be embarrassed she muttered a brief apology, stepped past him and knocked on the door.

It was opened immediately by a small dark-haired man.

"Miss Dawson? Please come this way,

Mr Watson is expecting you," he said, his accent indicating that he was neither English nor American.

Closing the door on a still fuming Frank, he led the way into a big, plain but luxuriously furnished sitting room.

"Please be seated, Miss Dawson. Mr Watson will be with you in a few moments."

He disappeared through another door and Pippa sank into a deep low leather chair. Thank goodness she had a few moments to calm herself. She had rarely had rows with Frank and to do so upset her, for he was undoubtedly fond of her. Did he love her? Was it what she thought of as love or was it nearer the same calm affection she had for him? He was possessive and kind and thoughtful, but rarely passionate. He had attempted to caress her intimately only a few times, and had always drawn back when she had repulsed him. Did that indicate lack of desire or gentlemanly consideration, she mused.

Before she could decide a question which she had often fruitlessly asked herself before, the other door opened and a tall, elderly man entered.

As he greeted her courteously Pippa studied him with interest. Although his white hair was receding from his high forehead and he was inclined to excess weight, he was still exceptionally good-looking, and his blue eyes were still bright and sharp. To her surprise he spoke with an American accent similar to her own.

"I had not realised that you came from the States," she said impulsively. "California?"

"I spent a great deal of time there," he replied. "Please sit over here by the window, Miss Dawson. I had the advantage, as my valet told me you were an American after he spoke to you on the telephone yesterday. Why do you want to bury yourself on a small Mediterranean island?" he added abruptly.

"I don't especially, but it would be interesting for a short time and your ad said a temporary job. I've never been out of the States before, so anywhere would be new and exciting," she added thoughtfully.

"You can type, and you are intelligent?" he demanded.

Pippa raised her eyebrows. "I can type," she said slowly. "I can judge that by results. It's not so easy to be sure I'm intelligent, though I hope I am!"

"Shorthand?"

"I'm afraid not. I didn't do a straight secretarial course, just added typing during my spare time at college. The ad didn't ask for it," she explained, a tinge of regret in her voice.

"It doesn't matter if you can transcribe direct from tapes. Let me explain the situation. For some years now I have been taping reminiscences with a view to publishing my memoirs. I have other notes in various notebooks, all out of any sort of order. I want someone to type them all up and then help me sort them into a sensible order. Could you do it?"

"It sounds quite a job," Pippa commented before she could stop herself, and then bit her lip and looked at him dubiously. He was laughing and she relaxed and grinned back at him.

"It will be. Does it sound interesting?"

"Yes, and I think I could cope. I've done a great deal of audio typing during vacations. I worked for my father mostly."

"Dawson? The law firm in L.A.?"

She nodded.

"Then you can be discreet as well, I presume? These memoirs are dynamite, I don't want snippets getting into the press before everything is ready."

"I can be trusted, Mr Watson."

"You would live in my villa. I have a Spanish couple there who cook and clean and drive me about. It's fairly isolated, but there's a pool and boats if that interests you, and I have a few acquaintances from the American communications base. No doubt you would soon acquire an escort. Otherwise there is little to do apart from look at prehistoric ruins, and there are plenty of them about. I would expect the job to last six months or so." He mentioned a monthly salary which made Pippa blink in surprise. Apart from the fact that she would have no living expenses it was higher than her father's personal secretary received.

"I'm only a beginner," she said doubtfully. "Do you think I'm worth that? And don't you want to take some references?"

"I'm paying you for confidentiality," he replied brusquely. "As for references, I never trust them. I think I'm a better judge of people than most. The job is yours if you want it. I would like to start at the end of next week."

"Yes please. And thank you," Pippa said firmly, casting the last lingering doubts about Frank behind her.

Mr Watson wrote swiftly on a sheet of paper from his pocket book.

"Here is the address and the phone number. I'm going back this weekend. Come out next Friday or Saturday, ring to let me know the time your plane arrives and I'll have Luis meet you at Mahon." He pulled out a cheque book and wrote swiftly. "Here, that should cover your air fare, use the rest to get clothes or books to amuse you. Goodbye, Miss Dawson, I look forward to a happy collaboration."

Before she could fully take in the fact that, unaided, she had landed herself a plum job with a huge salary Pippa found herself outside the suite, the cheque and

15

the paper with the address on clutched in her hand, her head still reeling from the suddenness of it all.

A few minutes later, totally unaware of how she had found her way there, she was standing outside the hotel entrance. She came back to earth at the sound of Frank's voice.

"Pippa!" he said pleadingly. "Darling, we must talk. Come and have lunch with me."

Pippa blinked and looked at him, then slowly shook her head.

"It's no good, Frank. It never was, I think."

"Don't say that. You're just angry with me and it's true I have no right to interfere, but I can't bear to lose you again. It has been bad enough being in London without you. I was so thrilled when you came here. I thought everything was settled, that you were happy about it and eager to see me again."

Pippa sighed.

"O.K., Frank, we'll have lunch but it won't alter my decision about the job. I've accepted it," she said flatly.

16

As they walked along to a quiet restaurant Frank knew, she wondered miserably whether, spurred on by her unusual bout of temper, she had been unfair to Frank. She had never previously given him reason to doubt her willingness to marry him. This morning's row had been a continuation of the one last night, when she had first voiced her doubts. It must have been a shock to him.

Suddenly contrite she took his hand as they crossed the road.

"I'm sorry, Frank."

"Then you'll change your mind?" he asked, stopping and taking her shoulders in his hands as he turned her to face him.

The furious hooting of a car made him release her hurriedly and drag her onto the narrow pavement, where he again turned her to face him. Pippa wriggled out of his grasp.

"Let's find lunch before talking, we can't concentrate here," she said as a group of people pushed past them and a delivery man balancing several cartons in his arms shouted to them to make way.

When they had ordered, Pippa took a

17

deep breath and looked at Frank. He was gazing at her hopefully and she had to steel herself to deal the hurtful blow.

"Frank, I don't know what I feel about us," she said slowly. "At the moment I don't think I love you well enough to get married. Perhaps, later, after I've been on my own a while — "

"We've been separated while I've been in London," he said quickly.

"I know, but it wasn't quite the same because I was at home with the family and all my friends. I didn't need you or I didn't feel that I did," she added as she saw the hurt in his eyes. "Oh dear, I'm making a rotten mess of this. I must make my own way for a time. I shall have time to think, to see whether I can be self-sufficient or whether I miss you unbearably."

"But I love you," he insisted.

"I know, and that's what makes me feel so mean. But I don't know what love is. I can't tell whether I love you. I need to find out, Frank, before I commit myself to marriage, because I believe marriage is for keeps. One has to be absolutely sure and I'm not."

"Do you have to do it so far away?" he asked.

"Yes, because anywhere in the States there would be the chance of you or Dad flying in for the weekend," she said frankly. "Or I could get home if I felt low. Anyway I've accepted the job and I can't let Mr Watson down. Besides, it sounds an exciting job, helping him write his memoirs."

"What's he like?" Frank demanded suspiciously.

"Old, you needn't be afraid I shall fall for him," she said with a slight laugh. "He's a Californian I think, or at least has lived there. He knew of Dad."

"Is he married?"

"I don't think so. He mentioned a Spanish couple who looked after him, there may be others, but I have the impression there's no wife."

"Will you be living in the same house? Your parents won't like that."

"Oh, don't be silly! He must be well over sixty and I'm not an idiot!" she snapped. "It's settled Frank. Now let's eat and talk about something else, and then I have to go and buy some guide

19

books and see about getting a flight."

To her relief he accepted this and she agreed to see him again that evening. Then she went to make enquiries of travel agents and in search of books about the Balearic Islands, thrusting to the back of her mind her doubts and the concern, mingled with slight irritation, at the hurt, bewildered expression in Frank's eyes.

During the next few days as she made preparations for her journey Frank's attitude was a constant worry. Why could she not love him as deeply as he plainly loved her?

"How can I tell?" she demanded one evening after Frank's alternated pleas and hurt silence had ruined her enjoyment of the film he had taken her to see.

"You'll know when it hits you," Dolores had reassured her. "If you don't want to spend every possible moment with Frank, and can't bear the thought of not spending the rest of your life with him, he's not the man for you. You don't love him, Pippa. You're just conditioned into accepting your family's wishes. You've probably never given any other possibility a thought."

That was true, Pippa silently agreed. Until she had come to England she had never really questioned the plans everyone had for her. The sudden independence of a trip abroad seemed to be encouraging her into other forms of rebellion also.

"Dad was livid when I phoned him," she commented. "He even threatened to come and fetch me home. I told him that if he did I would never marry Frank, but if I had some time on my own to think it over I might go back to him after all."

"You mustn't. He's not right for you, Pippa. Can you bear the way he is pleading, almost whining to you not to leave him?"

"He's hurt and it has been sudden," Pippa said defensively, but she had a sneaking feeling that Dolores was right.

"So what? I would respect a man who went away more than one who stayed to beg. Or one who acted the cave man and carried me off," she added, giggling. "Cheer up, Pippa, the job will last the next few months and anything may happen. Have you found out who your Mr Watson is and what sort of memoirs he's writing?"

"No. It was stupid of me not to ask him more. It's odd. I have a feeling I've seen him before somewhere but I can't think how or where. Well, I shall find out on Friday."

2

WHEN she was about to step into the small bus which took her out to the plane at Gatwick on Friday, however, Pippa almost turned back. What the devil am I doing, she asked herself in dismay. How can I be going off to a small island to work for a man I don't know, living in his house, making Frank so miserable, all for some whim about the need to find a job for myself?

She hesitated and then moved on. The last sight she had had of Frank's pleading eyes across the barrier decided her. Dolores was right. She didn't love him and the sooner he accepted it the better it would be for them both. When she did return home there would be no way of avoiding him permanently but in the meantime he might have accepted her decision. If she went back now he never would.

She had a seat by the small window,

and a young man carrying several expensive looking cameras squeezed into the seat beside her, giving her a brief smile as he began to stow away the cameras under the seat.

"There's so little room on these charter flights," he said as he sat up again, "but I daren't trust this stuff with the rest of the baggage."

"It is rather cramped," Pippa agreed, mentally contrasting the spacious luxury of the transatlantic flight with this one.

She had discovered that the cheapest and easiest way of getting to Mahon was on a package holiday flight. The agency had offered her a last minute bargain and her thrifty mind had made her accept eagerly. She was glad that it was only a two hour flight, though, in such a small cramped plane.

"Good, no hold up," her neighbour said as the doors were shut and the captain's voice filled the passenger cabin. They taxied along the runway and were soon airborne. Pippa gazed entranced as they passed over the towns and fields of southern England and then over the sea, the cliffs of Dover gleaming down on her left.

"Is that France?" she asked a few minutes later as they crossed another coast line.

"Yes, ever been there?"

"No, it's my first trip to Europe."

"And you choose to go to Minorca? Have you friends there?" he asked. "By the way, my name's David Nightingale."

"Pippa Dawson. Not friends, I'm going to work there for a few months."

"Tourist trade?"

"No, secretarial, for an American."

"Pity. I was hoping we might be staying in the same place."

He paused to speak to the stewardess who was distributing the plastic packed trays, and Pippa concentrated on seeing what she could of the French countryside with the meandering rivers and woods clearly visible before the plane rose into the clouds and they were surrounded by thin, floating cotton wool. Soon they were above the clouds, the sky brilliantly blue, and she sighed with satisfaction, at last happy that she was doing the right thing in leaving Frank in England.

David, having tossed her a few casual remarks as they ate, had produced a book from his pocket and was immersed in it. She saw that it was one of the guides she had herself bought and wished that she had thought to leave hers accessible. The paperback novel she had in her bag did not appeal at the moment, for it had reached the stage where the heroine was agonising over which man she loved most, and in Pippa's currently lovelorn state she had little patience with reading about a girl who thought that she could be in love with two men at once.

She was peering unobtrusively over David's shoulder at the map he was studying when he looked up at her and grinned.

"Where are you staying?" he queried as she blushed and began to apologise.

"Near the western end, somewhere close to here — I can't say the name," she replied, pointing.

"Cuidadela. The easiest way is to think of the C as Th, and that helps. Try it."

Pippa did, and after a few attempts which made her laugh, made a creditable pronunciation.

"Do you speak Spanish well?" she asked.

"Moderately. Enough to get by and ask the questions I want. My work, and therefore my vocabulary, is rather specialised."

"You are working?" Pippa asked in surprise.

"I'm doing the photographs and helping with some of the drawings for a book on the archeological remains. The whole island is littered with them and half of them still haven't been properly surveyed."

"Have you been before?"

"Not to Minorca. I went to Majorca, the largest of the group, recently. Minorca is further north and totally different. There are no mountains for a start, and the terrain is rocky, less fertile than in Majorca. No cultivated olives, and only a few orange trees in gardens. Majorca has hundreds of orchards."

"What is there, then?"

"Cattle mainly, and leather goods, especially shoes. Far fewer tourists which is an advantage for those of us who have to work. It's warmer than in London.

You'll soon need something lighter," he added, and cast a swift admiring glance at Pippa's trim pants suit in a fine dark red wool, under which she wore a cream sweater.

"I never learned Spanish despite living in California," she said hurriedly. "Do you think I'll be able to understand?"

"Lots of people speak some English," he reassured her. "The island has been occupied several times, the Arabs were here until the thirteenth century, then both the French and English spent some time in control during the eighteenth century, so the dialect is not pure Spanish, there are quite a few foreign words. I'll be happy to be your guide and interpreter when you have some time free," he added. "My base is here," he said, pointing to the map. "Cala Santa Galdana is perhaps the loveliest bay on the island, and although there are new hotels and houses it is still very pleasant. There's a good new road and it's not far from Cuidadela."

"There are no coast roads," Pippa remarked, evading replying to his implied invitation. She had found him a pleasant companion but after her rupture with Frank and the distress that had caused her did not wish to plunge straight into another friendship. If she relied on David Nightingale for company too much things could become difficult again.

"No, just this main road connecting the two capitals. Mahon is the modern one, mainly because it has a magnificent natural harbour, but Cuidadela was the original one. Most of the time to get from one part of the coast to another you have to come back to the main road. There are a few other roads connecting some of the resorts but the rest are mere tracks."

"You have done your homework to know so much already," Pippa said ruefully. "I skimmed through my guide books but I didn't learn nearly as much."

"Have you got this one?" David asked, and Pippa nodded.

"But I packed it in my case."

"Would you care to look at it now?"

"Thank you, but I'll wait to read my own when I'm settled. We should be there soon, I think."

"Another twenty minutes or so. Are you being met?"

"Yes. Mr Watson, my employer, said his chauffeur would be waiting for me. I hope I'll be able to spot him."

"I expect so, Mahon must be a very tiny airport."

"I've so little idea what to expect," Pippa confessed, and thought ruefully that this remark applied to more than just the size of the airport.

They landed soon afterwards and Pippa found it was an exceedingly small airfield. The plane taxied along the runway and drew up a few yards away from the incredibly small airport building, and the passengers were waiting within minutes for their cases to appear on the conveyor belt.

David's soon arrived and he heaved it to the floor.

"Look, I'll go and check if the hire car I ordered is waiting, then make sure you are met. I'll see you just outside," he said and walked off while Pippa waited for her own two cases. She looked after him, half wishing to call him back.

He was just under six feet tall, with short curly brown hair. Dressed in casual brown slacks with a darker brown sweater over a white tee-shirt, his slim figure looked confident and at ease as he spoke for a moment to the officials at the customs desk, showing them the cameras slung over his shoulder. By the time he had dealt with them Pippa had seen one of her cases on the belt, and as she turned to lift it off he disappeared. When her other case had been retrieved she carried them past the customs officers, who gave her a cursory glance and waved her through, to find David waiting immediately outside by the glass doors which opened onto a large car park.

"I suspect that chap is your chauffeur," he said, nodding to a small dark man in a smart green uniform. "Look, here's my hotel phone number. Ring me as soon as you can and I'll take you out as soon as you have a free day. I'll check that you're O.K."

So saying he picked up the larger of her cases and carried it across to the chauffeur, speaking to him rapidly in Spanish, and then turning to grin cheerfully at Pippa. She had already recognised the man who had been in London with Mr Watson.

"This is Luis, Pippa. See you soon, I hope. Good luck."

"Goodbye," she managed, and watched rather bereft as he waved and strode away to a small car some distance away.

"Miss Dawson, welcome to Minorca," Luis said in a heavily accented voice. "Please get in the car, I will see to your baggage. It is an hour to the Casa Blanca. There is a map in the door pocket so that you can see where we go."

Soon they were driving out from the airport past the outskirts of Mahon and along the central road. Pippa stared out at the stone walls, the fields littered with rocks and stones, and the scattered, white-painted houses.

There was little traffic on the road which had clearly been widened and improved in places recently. It went through the three inland towns of the island and the only stretch of low hills, but Pippa noticed one hill larger than the others standing alone near the centre of the island.

"That is the Sanctuary of Mount Toro," Luis explained in his precise English. "The church is kept by the nuns and is a popular attraction for visitors."

"How do they get to the top? Is there a road? It looks very steep."

"There is a twisting road, but only small buses can traverse it. A large coach which made the attempt once became stuck at one of the sharp turns."

"How unfortunate. What happened?" Pippa asked curiously.

"Oh, the driver had to reverse until he reached a quarry further down where he could turn round. The passengers all got out and walked up to the summit," Luis added, flashing her a grin which revealed even white teeth.

"I'm not surprised," Pippa laughed. "I would not like to be in a bus reversing along hairpin bends."

"You must visit it. Perhaps if the Senor stays he — oh, this is Mercadal where shoes are made from old car tyres and the skin of cattle. The islanders wear them in the fields, they last a very long time, they are so strong."

From Mercadal the road twisted more and soon after they had passed through Ferrarias, the next town, Luis turned the

33

car into a small lane, little better than a track, and drove towards the southern coast.

The lane was deep, enclosed either side with high stone walls edging the fields or dense plantations of pine trees, so Pippa could see little of the landscape. She gasped as the car left the last of these plantations and in front of her the blue sea glittered far below.

To either side stretched headland after headland of low grey cliffs, and as Luis began to drive carefully down a steep track she saw on her left a small deserted cove with a beach of golden sand and a scattering of low rocks at the edges of the cliffs.

"It belongs to the Casa Blanca," Luis said casually. "No-one else can reach it except by boat, so it is usually quite private. Do you swim?"

"Yes, but not very well," Pippa answered, gazing entranced at the variable green and brown and blue patches of water in the shallow bay.

"It is best for even a strong swimmer to stay within the bay, no further out than those two rocks on either side which curl inwards towards each other," Luis warned. "There can be a strong current outside."

At that moment the track curved and Pippa saw in front of her a long, low, white house set in the flat floor of the narrow valley, surrounded by lawns and flower beds. A large patio faced southwards, and on the upper storey wide balconies in front of green shuttered windows provided several sunbathing or lounging areas.

Luis drove into a paved space to the side of the house and brought the car to a halt near a porticoed entrance. The huge door stood open revealing a cool, spacious interior, with oriental rugs scattered across the cream tiled floor and modern paintings, bright and large, on the walls.

"I'll fetch Maria, my wife, to show you the room she has prepared for you," Luis said as he dropped Pippa's cases on to the hall floor at the foot of a wide curving staircase which filled the centre of the large hall that ran across the whole depth of the house. "Mr Watson is most likely resting and will see you before dinner."

He disappeared through a door beyond the staircase and Pippa looked about her with interest. Several doors opened to both sides of the hall, and dozens of potted plants were scattered about the room on the floor and tables and suspended from the ceiling. It added to the cool cream and green elegance, and just as the rugs and paintings provided vivid splashes of colour so did the blossoms and variegated leaves of the plants.

She then became aware of a murmur of voices coming as far as she could tell from a nearby room. It appeared that Mr Watson was not resting as Luis had supposed, and Pippa wondered whether she ought to make her presence known to whoever was in the room. Yet her new employer must have visitors and she did not wish to interrupt them. She stood irresolute, and at that moment a door beside her opened.

"I'll sue you for every cent, Gene, if you insist on publishing that rubbish!" a low husky voice said, and Pippa stepped away from the door, startled at the venom in the voice.

A man laughed abruptly.

"To do that successfully, my dear Sally-Jayne, you'd have to disprove what I say, and that would be difficult with regard to our private dealings!"

It was Mr Watson, a note of amusement in his tone. Clearly, Pippa thought, the conversation was to do with the memoirs she had been employed to help organise. Who was the woman, she wondered, and what sort of memoirs could they be to stimulate such anger?

"I could reveal some pretty discreditable things about you if I chose!" the woman continued and then a third voice, teasingly familiar to Pippa's ears, spoke decisively.

"There is nothing to be gained by either of you indulging in such petty recriminations," the man said. "I cannot see any reason for giving the gossips more scandal to chew over, Gene. Why are you so determined to publish?"

"I want to set the record straight," Mr Watson, who must be Gene, Pippa realised as she looked impotently about her for a way of avoiding this embarrassing conversation, said curtly.

"Is it worth stirring up old hatreds and creating new ones?"

"Your name would be mud after I'd finished," the woman interjected.

"I've been maligned often enough in the past. This will be my version. As to you, my dear, since the doctors give me no more than a year why should I care about the calumnies that will be thrown at me? They will not disturb me."

"If that does not concern you why should the record do so?"

"That will remain long after the gossip has been forgotten, Juan."

"Then you won't reconsider?" the woman asked, and after a brief silence she gave an exclamation of fury and the door was opened wide.

Pippa, wishing that she could disappear into some of the greenery in the hall, stepped back still further from the door, but the woman who emerged did not see her for as soon as she had gained the hall she turned abruptly to face the man who had followed her out.

She was tall, golden haired, and one of the most beautiful women Pippa had ever seen. She wore a sleeveless, plunging white top and a brief white skirt which showed to great advantage her tanned skin and long, shapely legs. Her figure was slender but voluptuous, and she moved with sinuous grace even though she was plainly in a furious temper.

"Can't you deal with the old fool, Juan?" she demanded, making no attempt to lower her voice so that Mr Watson would not hear.

Pippa did not hear his reply because a harsh laugh from inside the room rose above the other voice, then the man came into view.

Pippa's eyes widened in surprise and just at that moment the man saw her. It was the same man she had twice collided with at the hotel in London when she had been going for her interview with Mr Watson. Confused by his contemptuous stare she recalled that on the second occasion it had been just outside the door of Mr Watson's suite, and it could have been quite probable that he had been coming away from it.

Before she could collect her wits together he spoke directly to her.

"So you are here. I trust you

39

found your eavesdropping rewarding," he said scathingly, and before she could indignantly deny the charge he had followed the woman to the outer door. As she stared after them she heard footsteps on the tiles of the hall and turned to see Luis, accompanied by a small plump woman, approaching.

"Maria will show you your room," Luis said and stood aside with Pippa's cases while his wife, smiling and nodding, led Pippa up the stairs, still fuming at the beastly, arrogant man's accusation.

They had reached the upstairs hall when they heard the sound of a car, and from the way in which Maria glanced at Luis, shrugging her shoulders, Pippa guessed that they were aware of Mr Watson's recent visitors.

Then she forgot the strange scene below as she exclaimed in wonder at the huge bedroom Maria led her to. A soft blue carpet covered the floor, and the curtains and a pair of comfortable armchairs were in a deeper shade. The bed was a low double divan with an exquisite snowy white lace bedspread. The walls too were white, and the bathroom glimpsed through an open door had white tiles and a bath in the same deep blue as the bedroom curtains.

"I will open the shutters, the sun is less hot now," Maria said and Pippa went to look out of the window as she did so.

On the balcony outside was a small table and several chairs, a lounger and a big adjustable sunshade, at present furled. The windows faced the beach and a small clump of pine trees hid one arm of the cliffs from view.

"It is beautiful, no?" Maria asked. "I will unpack your cases now while Luis tells Mr Watson that you have arrived."

Pippa nodded absently. She had seen an open topped Mercedes snaking its way along the track out of the valley, and she recalled with mingled fury and puzzlement the antagonism displayed by the unknown man. She had met him so briefly, three times, yet on each occasion she had appeared in a bad light. First she had been absorbed in contemplating her reflection in the hotel mirror. She wanted to justify her apparent vanity by explaining that any girl facing an interview for a job wanted to look her best. Then he had heard her angry argument with Frank outside Mr Watson's suite and must have formed an even worse impression of her, unaware that Frank had pursued her against her wishes and had persisted in arguing with her. And finally he had found her apparently listening to a conversation which could be none of her business.

"Though what I could have done about it, not knowing the house, I can't think!" she said indignantly, and shook her head in response to Maria's enquiring look. "Sorry, I have a bad habit of talking to myself," she said with an embarrassed laugh. "Who were the people with Mr Watson when I arrived?"

Maria gave her a strange look.

"Il Conde Juan is his nephew, his sister's child. She married a Spanish nobleman," she explained. "The other was Sally-Jayne Ross, his last wife."

"Sally-Jayne Ross? The actress?" Pippa asked in astonishment.

"Did you not recognise her?" Maria asked, surprised.

Pippa thought of the famous blonde

beauty, noted for her green eyes and ravishing smile, and accepted it suddenly.

"I had a feeling that she was familiar," she admitted. "I've seen her in her last two films. But I didn't know she was married to Mr Watson."

"She is not now," Maria said drily, "but she often stays on Mallorca and a fast boat can soon bring her here."

"Mallorca? Oh yes, that is the Spanish name for the larger island," Pippa said with a smile. "I shall have to use it. You speak such good English, Maria."

"I lived in London when I was a girl, my family had a famous restaurant there. I married Luis when he was there with Mr Watson and have spent years in California until Mr Watson gave up acting."

"Acting? Then he — Mr Watson was also in films?" she asked, astonished.

Maria smiled suddenly. "You are not very quick to recognise stars, Miss Dawson," she said with a laugh. "Perhaps it is to be understood if you were not expecting to meet them. Mr Watson's name in Hollywood was Gene Perrier. Did he not tell you that the book he plans to write is all about his years in the film business?"

"No, he did not!" Pippa said, startled. Gene Perrier, she was thinking in amazement. One of the best known actors of thirty or forty years ago, he had never been a great star, but he had played major roles in many of the best and most popular films, and many critics had maintained that he had never been given the opportunity of showing his real potential in leading parts. Rumours of his blunt manner and outspokenness towards other actors and directors were rife in his heyday, and Pippa had read that this had prevented him from reaching the very top. Was he bitter, vindictive against those he might have disagreed with? Did he intend to publish his version of what had happened? From the few sentences she had just overheard it seemed likely. Her task as his assistant would prove rather more exciting than she had imagined, Pippa realised.

Maria had been speaking and Pippa came to with a start.

"I'm sorry, what did you say?" she apologised.

"I'll go and ask whether Mr Watson is ready to see you now," Maria said and left the room.

Pippa sat down on one of the balcony chairs, staring out over the sea. She did not look at the rippling waves, stirred by a slight breeze, however. In her mind she saw the look of contempt on the face of the man she had encountered on three brief occasions, three times when he had caught her in actions which could appear detrimental to herself. He must have been visiting his uncle at the hotel in London, she realised, for she had seen him the second time right outside the suite. He must have emerged while she was arguing with Frank. Juan, Maria had called him. Il Conde. That must be the same as Count.

Would she see him again, Pippa wondered. Would she have the opportunity of changing the impression he had already formed of her? Vain, bad tempered, and unduly curious, that must be the way he thought of her, and she was none of those horrid things. Without wondering why she longed for the chance to prove his first impressions wrong.

3

ARIA soon returned and took
Pippa down to a large and
sumptuously furnished sitting
room. The floor was of highly polished
parquet with scattered white wool rugs,
and deep green leather armchairs. Three
pairs of wide french windows opened
onto the patio and the curtains, white
flowers on a green background, moved
sinuously in the slight breeze.

Mr Watson was seated in a chair near
one of the windows, his hands clasping
a brandy goblet. He smiled at Pippa as
Maria ushered her into the room.

"Please forgive me, Miss Dawson, if I
remain seated. I have not been well these
past few days. Come and sit down."

He looked pale and drawn and Pippa
felt a sudden anger against the couple
who, seeing him like this, had still
importuned him about his memoirs.

"Can I do anything?" she asked in
concern as she perched on the arm of

46

another leather chair opposite him.

"Pour me another brandy if you will," he said, draining the goblet of the last few drops it held and holding it out to her. "It's all right Maria, you can go back to the kitchen. Miss Dawson will take good care of me as you see."

Maria nodded, gave Pippa an anxious smile as she crossed to the table holding the decanters, and softly left the room, although Pippa noted that she did not quite close the door behind her.

"Help yourself to a sherry while you're there, or anything else you fancy," Mr Watson suggested. "The sherry is very good, my nephew grows it on his estates."

Pippa poured the drinks and carried them back to where he sat.

"Your nephew?" she queried. "He is Spanish?"

"Rather more than half, in effect. One of my grandparents was Spanish and my sister, Juan's mother, married a Spaniard. You may have seen him, he has just left."

"Er — yes, I did see him briefly," Pippa agreed.

"He is staying here with me at the moment, but I believe he intends to take a boat across to Majorca and no doubt will spend the night there," Mr Watson said and a bitter note crept into his voice.

"Are the islands far apart?" Pippa asked.

"The shortest distance is about twenty-five miles, so it does not take long in a fast motor boat. Slightly more to Puerto Pollensa or Formentor and twice as long to Palma, although Juan rarely goes to the capital, he prefers the quieter areas. Do you like the sherry?"

"I've never tasted sherry so smooth and rich," Pippa replied. "Does your nephew produce much?"

"Not a great deal, his estate near Jerez is small. The main ones are near Malaga where the wine is first class, and Toledo where vast quantities of cheap wine is grown in the La Mancha area."

Pippa blinked. The nephew must be wealthy with three estates producing these various wines. She wondered what his attitude to herself would be when he returned. He clearly disliked the notion of his uncle's memoirs being published and he already was contemptuous of her. Was the bitterness she had discerned in Mr Watson's voice simply because of this opposition or had it some other cause?

She had no time to muse further for Mr Watson was talking again.

"I'm going to ask you to excuse me a moment, Miss Dawson. I have a weak heart and think it best if I retire to bed before dinner. Tomorrow morning I will show you the tapes and my notes, then I usually rest in the afternoon. You are welcome to take the Seat and explore the island any afternoon, or swim if the heat is not too much for you. Probably not if you are accustomed to Californian weather. We'll spend each morning checking over what you have typed and if you can spend an hour or so at some time during the afternoon or evening typing we should have plenty to work on. Please will you ring the bell for Luis? He will serve your dinner later after he has helped me to bed."

Pippa had already seen the ornate bell rope hanging beside a white marble fireplace and she crossed to tug at it.

Luis appeared almost immediately and assisted his master to rise and cross the room. As they went out Pippa stood irresolute, wondering whether to remain or return to her bedroom, but before she could decide Maria came in.

"Will you eat in the dining room or your bedroom?" she asked.

"I don't want to be any trouble to you. Would it be easier if I had a tray in my room?"

"It is still warm enough in the evening to sit on your balcony," Maria suggested. "We keep American rather than Spanish hours so dinner is almost ready. Luis will soon have finished helping Mr Watson and then he will bring up a tray to your room. Mr Watson's room is at the end down here, by the way, he finds stairs too much for his heart. Can you find your way back to your room?"

Pippa reassured her, and made her way slowly back upstairs. Mr Watson had not looked ill in London and she wondered whether his weakness today had been caused by the advent of his former wife and the argument she had inadvertently overheard. A sudden wave of anger against the lovely Sally-Jayne made her grind her teeth together, and she determined that she would do her utmost to protect her employer from further such intrusions.

After a delicious meal and a peaceful night's sleep Pippa rose the next morning full of energy. She showered and put on a simple cotton dress of pale yellow, trimmed with white collar and pockets and a narrow white belt. She fixed some chunky white earrings in her ears and slipped on matching yellow sandals, then made her way downstairs. Sounds of movement took her to a room at the back of the house, beside the front door, where she found Maria laying a table for two beside a large open window through which the bright morning sun streamed.

"I hope you slept well," Maria greeted her, smiling. "Mr Watson is much better this morning and will be with you in a moment. Help yourself, if you please. Everything is on the side table."

She went out and Pippa poured herself some fresh orange juice and carried it to the window where she stood sipping it as she looked out.

The paved open space was surrounded by flowering shrubs beyond which the hillside rose gradually away from the sea. To the right were massive iron scrolled gates hung on stone pillars, but they stood wide open and Pippa suspected that they were never closed. On the left, through another stone archway and more gates she glimpsed outbuildings, and the car in which Luis had collected her from Mahon stood before what must be a garage, although she thought that further on there were stable doors.

She finished her orange and went to pour coffee. Carrying that and a hot fresh croissant she returned to the table and had just seated herself when Mr Watson came into the room.

"Don't get up, Miss Dawson. I'm feeling much better today, fit for lots of work."

He did look much better, his colour had returned and the strain had disappeared from his face, Pippa thought, and smiled as he sat down opposite her with juice and coffee.

"I hope you slept well, Miss Dawson?"

"Like a top, thank you. I'm so glad you

feel better Mr Watson. I was worried last night."

"I'm sorry your reception was rather brief. Look, may I call you Pippa? Miss Dawson is so formal and I've never been accustomed to much formality. I'd prefer you to call me Gene if you don't mind, too. Everyone else does apart from Maria and Luis, they won't abandon Spanish formality."

"Pippa sounds better for me," she replied with a laugh. "Miss Dawson sounds so old, I'll never get used to it."

"I doubt if you'll have to, you'll be bound to marry soon and take your husband's name unless, that is, you're one of these so-called emancipated women who clings to spurious independence."

Pippa blushed and shook her head.

"It must make it very complicated for the children," she commented.

"Indeed. I had no children apart from a daughter who was killed in a riding accident when she was ten — many years ago," he said quietly. "Of course actresses keep their own names for professional reasons but privately have taken my name. I've been married to three actresses," he added with a slight frown. "I think now that to marry into the same profession is a mistake, but I never tried anything else and now it's too late."

"Will your memoirs be about Hollywood mainly?" Pippa asked after a brief silence.

"About my career? Yes, and also about my marriages, because they were linked with it, inevitably. I hope you are not a prude or squeamish, Pippa? Some of what I have to say is blunt and on occasion when I was carried away the language I used on the tapes was somewhat colourful!"

Pippa laughed. "I won't be shocked," she reassured him. "My father frequently forgot himself."

"I shall have to change that for publication. Type in stars or something if you prefer not to be totally accurate. Have you had enough? Then let's start."

He led the way out of the room and along to another one past the kitchens, which were near the central stairs.

"This is my study at the back of the house where it is shady and has no view of the sea to distract me. I was born in Maryland and spent most of my boyhood on boats of some sort. That is why I built on an island, I think, when I decided to retire."

He spent the next hour showing Pippa where he kept his tapes, several dozen of them, and a drawerful of closely filled notebooks.

"I dated the entries in the books, usually, but more often forgot when I taped things. But I did finish one tape before starting the next so it should not be impossible to deduce when I made them. But they are mixed in content, I tended to jump from one thing to another as recalling one episode reminded me of others. Does it sound impossible?"

"Not if you can date the incidents described," Pippa said cheerfully, although the sheer amount of the material had rather daunted her.

"Here is my new toy, a word processor," Gene said proudly. "It is easy to use, I've already discovered, and you can store whatever you type, print it out for us to work on, two copies or more, and then rearrange as we go."

"I've never used one," Pippa said, aghast. "Shouldn't you have advertised for someone who knows how to operate one?"

"Every typist will have to learn some day. It really is not difficult. Look, there's a good book of instructions and you will only need a few of the simpler ones to begin with."

He demonstrated how to set up the machine and how to store the typed information on slim disks, then selected a tape and put it into the player.

"I need some air while it is still fairly cool, Pippa. I'll leave you to experiment for an hour or so and then we'll have lunch."

Pippa had made the first tentative trials on the word processor and was poring over the instruction book when Maria brought in some coffee.

"Oh, thank you, Maria," she said, glancing at her watch. "I hadn't realised the time had gone so quickly. I'm trying to make sense of this thing. It sounds marvellous if only I can sort it all out."

Maria sniffed. "Mr Watson loves gadgets, we have every new type in the kitchen," she commented. "If you get stuck Il Conde Juan will help you, he is an expert on computers and such."

"I thought he was a wine producer," Pippa said, surprised.

"So is every Spanish landowner in the vine growing areas," Maria responded. "What else would they do? Il Conde has a large business making these gadgets, in America," she explained. "That is his real interest, the vineyards are only what he inherited from his father."

She went out and Pippa sat back to enjoy her coffee. She switched on the tape, feeling ready to begin typing but wishing to listen to the tape first. Gene's voice filled the room, a full strong actor's voice, and she hastily turned down the volume.

For a moment the words did not make sense and she realised that she had the second side of the tape. She let it run through, gradually picking up the threads of the story Gene was relating. It concerned some dubious sounding financial deal made by the president of an international company and one of the large film studios, and had a

57

great deal to do with a young starlet in whom the president appeared to have a romantic interest.

"Whew!" Pippa said softly as the recording ended. If all Gene's revelations were of such a nature the memoirs would create one of the greatest scandals for years.

She turned the tape to the beginning and began to transcribe, finding the word processor keyboard easy and pleasant to use. By the time Gene returned and Maria announced lunch she was feeling quite confident that she would be able to manage it. It was only Gene's laughing command that she was to spend the afternoon out of doors or resting that dissuaded her from practising her new skills all afternoon.

"Go and swim, or walk up to the headland," Gene suggested. "The bay is as private as it can be apart from when boats come in exploring, and there are no houses on the coast for some distance. The farms were built inland for shelter and protection against Moorish raids. The nearest is a mile away along the valley."

So Pippa spent the afternoon lazing on the beach, and after a swim in the surprisingly cold water went back to sit on her balcony writing letters home.

She started one to Frank and then paused. Ought she to give him the slightest encouragement to hope? She was becoming more and more certain that she would never marry him but to send him friendly letters as soon as she had arrived in her new job could give him the wrong impression. She screwed up the sheet and began another letter to Dolores, then exclaimed in annoyance as a stray gust of wind blew the screwed up paper off the table and it floated down into the garden.

It was almost time for dinner so Pippa changed out of the shorts she had worn on the beach into a cool apple green dress, slim and flattering to her figure, making her appear taller and feel sophisticated. She brushed her curls which had become springier after her swim and the quick shampoo she had given them as she had a shower, and wished for the hundredth time that she looked less youthful. Straight hair would, she had often thought, enable her to seem more sophisticated, and she envied women who could sweep up their hair into smooth rolls or cut it to give a sculpted look to their heads.

She opened the door into the sitting room and then paused. Gene was seated in his favourite chair but standing by one of the windows, looking out over the bay, was his nephew. Pippa had not heard him return and was unprepared to face this man who must have such an unflattering impression of her.

The Count, however, gave her a friendly smile and walked across the room to meet her.

"You must be Miss Dawson," he said calmly. "Juan y Correa, at your service."

Pippa straightened her shoulders and raised her chin as she turned towards him, and he eyed her appreciatively.

"Welcome to the Casa Blanca," he went on smoothly. "I am happy to make your acquaintance."

She raised her eyebrows sceptically and his lips twitched slightly as he took her hand in his and drew her towards him. For a moment she thought that he intended to raise it to his lips and she stiffened involuntarily. He was not going to make her forget his previous unflattering comments by using his obvious charm, the effect of which he was no doubt fully conscious. His fingers tightened over hers and he led her across to the drinks table.

"What will you drink?"

"She likes your sherry, Juan," Gene interposed with a slight laugh. "Come and sit down, Pippa. Did you enjoy your swim?"

"Yes, thank you, although the water was colder than I had expected."

"It doesn't get really warm until next month. You haven't seen the heated pool yet, then?" the Count asked, bringing a glass of sherry across to Pippa. She took it, careful to avoid touching his long, slender fingers.

"No. I recall now you said something about a pool, Gene, in London."

"It is to the side of the house opposite the main door. Small but always warm. I usually take a dip in the morning if I am feeling well enough. The doctors permit me that exertion, and walking."

"You must take it easy, Gene," the Count said. "I shall depend on Miss Dawson to see that you do not exert yourself too much on this new project, if you really are determined to go ahead."

Luis then announced dinner and the Count helped his uncle to rise from the deep chair, and offered him his arm as they went towards the door.

"No, I can manage, Juan. Look after Pippa for me."

The Count turned to look at Pippa, a steady close regard that made her suddenly tremble nervously. Hesitantly she took the proffered arm and went through to the formal dining room which opened from the sitting room and was furnished in a similar style.

"Thank you, sir," Pippa said in a strained voice as the Count held her chair for her, and he laughed softly.

"Call me Juan, if you please, and pray permit me to address you as Pippa. If my uncle claims that privilege I will do so too."

He smiled deep into her eyes as he bent over her, then moved away to seat himself opposite while Gene sat at the head of the polished walnut table, set with gleaming silver and spotless white napery.

Pippa fumed silently. How self possessed, almost complacent, he was she thought to herself. And why, when he so clearly resented the work she was doing and thought her conceited and sly, was he taking such pains to be friendly? She responded to his remarks with as cool a detachment as she could contrive, although she was certain he was inwardly laughing at her.

Luis served the meal expertly and Pippa did full justice to the delicious fish soup, followed by goulash, a selection of French cheeses and fresh fruit. Gene drank sparingly of the excellent wines but he took a full glass of brandy when they returned to the sitting room. Juan opened the doors of a discreet cupboard to reveal a modern, elaborate set of stereo equipment, and selected a record of classical guitar music which had, he explained to Pippa, been made recently by a friend of his.

She listened intently, marvelling at the skill of the artist, and lost in the haunting, evocative melodies. Then the tempo changed suddenly and she found her feet tapping to the rhythm of the traditional flamenco dancing.

"Have you seen our Spanish dancers?" Juan asked, and she came out of her abstraction with a start.

"No, never, apart from briefly in some film. I forget which."

"Perhaps you would give me the pleasure of your company one evening and I will take you to see some local performers," he suggested.

"Good idea, Juan. I've been afraid Pippa would find it lonely here," Gene said, and before Pippa could object she found the two men calmly making plans for her to dine with Juan on the following evening and see a visiting troupe of dancers who were performing at one of the larger hotels in Cuidadela.

Pippa lay awake for some time longing for the courage to repudiate the arrangement. Angrily she recalled the various looks of disdain or amusement she had seen on the Count's face, and shivered with apprehension at the thought of being alone with him. She had never met anyone so cool and sophisticated before, she realised, who moved in the highest circles of European nobility and American industrialists and film moguls. He would be sure to find her gauche and provincial and thoroughly boring, when he was not being contemptuous of her shortcomings or laughing at her. She squirmed with helpless fury at being subjected to his closer scrutiny.

The Count was not visible at breakfast, and Gene told her that he had taken out a sailing boat long before either of them had risen.

"He said that he would expect you to be ready at eight. Now, how are you getting on with my infernal machine?"

Pippa laughed. "I think I shall soon pick it up. I can store data and operate the printer, and it's wonderful to be able to correct mistakes so easily. I should be able to do quite a lot today."

"Good. I want to go through my files, there are several letters that I would like to read again to refresh my memory, so I'll see to that and keep out of your way. We'll have coffee together on the patio and compare progress."

That morning Pippa did a considerable amount of typing and after lunch she wandered up onto the headland. The ground was sparsely covered with low bushes and a few straggling trees, and on the far side of the headland she found a small rocky cove and a tiny sandy beach. The next headland was higher, and at the end the rock had been eaten away to form a narrow archway leading through, at a place a few feet below the waterline, into what looked like a much larger bay.

She stared out to sea. A few sails were visible and she wondered whether one of the boats belonged to the count, but they were all too far away for her to distinguish the occupants. Again she wondered why she had permitted him to date her and was tempted to plead the excuse of a headache.

That would be cowardly, she told herself firmly. Why should I be afraid? He cannot harm me and he was pleasant last night, whatever his opinion of her was. It occurred to her that he might have agreed to Gene's suggestion because he saw it as an opportunity to persuade

Pippa against his uncle's project. But she would not be influenced by that, she thought scornfully.

Nevertheless she was restless and went back to the house and changed into a sleek white bathing suit, then found her way to the heated pool where she swam several lengths until she felt exhausted.

She was floating on her back, her eyes closed against the bright sun, when she heard footsteps approaching along the patio. They turned the corner of the house and there was silence as the paving gave way to grass. Pippa looked up to find the Count staring down at her, an amused smile on his face.

"Is it more comfortable than the sea?" he enquired, and Pippa spluttered as she let herself sink into the water when she opened her mouth to reply.

As she surfaced she found his hand stretched down towards her and grasped it while she coughed out the water she had swallowed.

"Come out," he ordered, and instinctively she obeyed the note of authority in his voice and reached up towards his other hand.

With apparently little effort he hauled her out of the water onto the surrounding grass, where she sat looking up at him in sudden confusion, for he was inspecting her shapely curves with obvious enjoyment.

"I must go and change," she said, struggling to her feet, but before she could escape his hand had captured one of hers again.

"Stay a while. It is hot, you will not suffer. I've asked Maria to bring out some beer. Please join me."

She looked at him doubtfully, an uncertain frown in her eyes.

"I trust you do not feel embarrassed, sitting here alone with me?" he added smoothly, grinning at her as she blushed hotly.

"I am surprised you should wish for my company when you think so badly of me!" she retorted with spirit. "And there is no need for you to obey Gene and take me out," she added, "for I do not expect to be squired about by you."

"Think badly of you?" he queried, ignoring the second part of her comment. "Why should I do that?"

Pippa was beginning to wish she had not started this topic of conversation, for his eyes were far too keen as he stared into hers.

"In London you thought I was conceited," she said at last.

He laughed, a deep, resonant sound.

"Not at all — just properly appreciative of a delightful picture. Come, sit down beside me. I do not bite."

"And you accused me of eavesdropping," she went on hurriedly. "That was unjust for I could not help overhearing what I did the day I arrived! I certainly had no wish to. I want nothing except to do my job properly, I am not concerned with anything else."

He looked at her ruefully, his eyes twinkling in amusement.

"I apologise humbly. I was angry, distraught, and worried about Gene, but it was unforgiveable of me to take it out on you. I hope you will show your forgiveness by joining me now for a beer and enduring my company tonight. It is not a duty to me, I assure you. I have every wish to enjoy your company."

Pippa was not at all sure that she

wanted to go out with this aggravating, disturbingly arrogant man, but she could not reject his apology without seeming churlish. She subsided onto the grass beside him. He grinned approvingly and then turned to stare out towards the sea, an abstracted look in his eyes. Pippa was able to examine him closely. Dressed in a white short sleeved shirt, open at the neck, and close fitting white jeans, his muscular limbs were obvious.

He was decidedly handsome, Pippa told herself, with his finely moulded bones and dark skin, and the contrasting brilliantly blue eyes. Sitting sideways she noticed a scar a couple of inches long just behind his ear, visible where his hair, windswept from his sailing, had been disarranged. She had a sudden urge to place her finger on the white scar tissue and felt herself colouring as he suddenly turned towards her.

He raised an eyebrow slightly, but before he could speak Maria appeared with a tray and beer and glasses. Making a business of pouring the beer for them both, Pippa sought desperately for a safe topic of conversation.

"You grow vines, Gene says, in several parts of Spain. Why are the wines different from each other?"

"Many reasons, the soil, the types of grape, the climate and the treatment once they are picked," he said, looking at her with a glint of amusement in his eyes as if he knew full well that she had seized on the topic merely to avoid more personal conversation.

He went on to describe the process of cultivation and Pippa found herself genuinely interested.

"It is a pity that there are no longer vineyards on Minorca, but one day I hope to be able to show you my own."

Pippa thought that most unlikely and soon afterwards made her escape on the plea that she ought to spend a couple of hours typing for his uncle before preparing to go out that evening.

She found it difficult to concentrate on the screen before her, however, for the Count's handsome face and the eyes that glinted with amusement at her discomfort or roved appreciatively over her almost naked body kept interposing themselves between her and the words she had

71

typed. Eventually she abandoned the attempt to concentrate and went to her room to select a suitable outfit for the evening.

She had two long evening gowns and a couple of short dresses suitable for dining out. She determined on the simplest short outfit, a long sleeved blue silk dress and then, when she was almost ready, thought that it would not be dressy enough for a date with a Count.

In somewhat of a panic she changed into a red ball gown, overlaid with white lace, which she had worn to formal college affairs. It was cut low across the bosom, with tiny puff sleeves and a full skirt. She surveyed herself in the mirror then suddenly began to wriggle out of the gown. It was far too revealing, far too elaborate for a simple dinner date. Casting it on the bed she took her other long dress, a plain sheath with a high neckline in a gold and brown figured material, from the wardrobe and began to scramble into it.

At last, somewhat breathless, she was ready. She slipped on gold sandals, clasped a gold bracelet about her arm, and picked up her gold filigree evening bag. It was ten past eight.

The Count, who was calmly sitting in the drawing room sipping sherry, did not seem aware of her lateness and poured her a sherry without asking her preference.

"You look very pretty, Pippa," Gene said admiringly, and Pippa smiled nervously at him. "Wish I was young enough to take you out myself," he added.

"You have Pippa to yourself during working hours," the Count said lightly. "I claim a share of her attention. Are you ready, Pippa?"

Pippa gulped the rest of her sherry and he came across to take the glass from her hand. Momentarily their fingers touched and she shivered. She glanced up into his face and her eyes met his. The expression in them was strange, enigmatic, and then suddenly he smiled and her heart began beating faster, and she was unable to breathe.

"Come," he murmured, taking her arm. "Good night, Gene."

"Good night, Juan. Have a good time,

Pippa, and stay late in bed tomorrow if you are late getting home."

Pippa made some response but she could not say what it had been. As if in a dream she walked out of the house with Juan, feeling herself as weak as a puppet and as completely at the mercy of the man who held her arm and guided her to the car waiting at the foot of the steps. The strange feeling did not leave her until, on reaching the outskirts of Cuidadela, the Count began to speak again and tell her details of the history of the old capital of the island.

4

THE Count was obviously well known at the restaurant, and Pippa was conscious of many curious eyes following their progress to a discreetly positioned table which had an excellent view of the small stage. Two women dining in other parts of the room waved and tried to catch his attention, but apart from a courteous bow Juan did not linger.

With the head waiter hovering, Juan ordered, choosing some Spanish specialities.

"You must taste some of the delicious cuisine of my country," he said softly to Pippa, leaning across towards her in a manner which suggested, she thought a trifle crossly, that he was paying her some extravagant compliment.

She happened to glance across at one of the women who had waved to Juan earlier and surprised a look of intense hatred in the woman's eyes. Then her companion spoke to her sharply and she hunched a shoulder and ostentatiously turned her chair so that her back was towards them.

"Who is that?" Pippa asked impulsively, then blushed as Juan smiled slightly, casting her a look of amusement.

"You mean the lady who is behaving somewhat petulantly?" he queried. "She is married to — and bored by — a Majorcan hotelier, and tries to console herself for his lack of appreciation of her opulent charms with demanding the praises of every other man she knows."

"Is that her husband?"

"Of course not. She is not the type who would be seen out with her own husband when someone else's is available."

His tone was contemptuous but Pippa thought she detected a note of anger too. Had he previously been one of the lady's escorts? Had they quarrelled? Was he annoyed with her or jealous? And was the woman angry merely on seeing him or resentful at the notice he was paying to herself?

She had to turn her attention to the

fresh lobster placed before her, and was savouring the first forkful when a husky voice spoke nearby in a drawling American accent.

"Darling! How long have you been in Minorca? Why didn't you tell me? Are you staying with Gene?"

A tall, slender redhead wearing a daringly low cut gown, was standing beside Juan, her hand stretched out towards him. He touched it briefly and stood up politely, forced to stand close to her as she did not move away to give him more room. The redhead, ignoring Pippa, began to issue a stream of invitations to luncheon parties, swimming and boating expeditions.

"And you must come to our barbecue on Saturday. Usual time darling, and dancing all night if you've the stamina," she added, and chuckled, casting Juan a mischievous glance from under mock-demure eyelids.

"Thank you, Liz, but I am not certain yet how long I can stay. Allow me to present Miss Pippa Dawson, from California, who is a friend of mine. Pippa, von Hauptmann."

The redhead inclined her head briefly towards Pippa.

"Do persuade him to come, Miss Dawson, if you are still here. There are heaps of old acquaintances longing to see him again."

She smiled up into Juan's eyes for a long moment and then moved away. Looking amused Juan resumed his seat.

"Liz is a glutton for parties," he commented. "If she does not either give or attend five or six a week she feels starved. She has outdistanced three husbands already, who have not had equal stamina."

Pippa smiled briefly. She was oddly grateful to him for introducing her as a friend, not merely an employee of his uncle's, and then it occurred to her that he might not wish it to be known that he had escorted his uncle's secretary on a social occasion. He certainly would not wish to introduce her to his wealthy friends. It must have been awkward for him to find two such dining in the same restaurant.

She had little time for brooding on this, however, as the dancers then came onto the stage. The girls, in red and white dresses, performed the stately traditional dances of flirtation and rejection while the haunting music filled the room, and their suitors enacted pleas and threats and despair.

The climax of the dancing came with Carmen, the leading dancer, dressed in a close fitting black gown which flared out below her knees to reveal a scarlet petticoat, matching the scarlet lipstick and the rose pinned into her hair, the only splashes of colour about her, performing a dance of such power and controlled passion that half of the diners were on their feet demanding more when it came to an end.

Carmen, unsmiling, acknowledged their applause gravely but refused every appeal for an encore. She and her partner left the stage and the excited diners returned to their forgotten food, while a sole guitarist played gentle, soothing music and the restaurant returned to normal.

"That was marvellous!" Pippa breathed. "I had not realised it could be so — expressive, so dramatic."

"The Spanish are passionate people," he remarked. "As I am not wholly Spanish I can share their characteristics and also, I believe, view them objectively. We love and hate with great intensity, which is not always wise."

He was staring down into his wine and Pippa wondered what he was thinking. What lay behind those words? Was he himself aware of loving unwisely? Before she could reply he looked up at her and her heart gave a sudden leap, whether of fear or some other emotion she could not decide.

"My uncle's memoirs, for instance. He has so little Spanish blood but the revelations he proposes to make of unbridled passions, of lust and fury and the intrigues they cause, will revive memories better left to slumber."

Pippa murmured something un intelligible. She could not defend Gene for as yet she knew very little of what he proposed to include in his memoirs, neither could she agree with Juan even if she had wished to. Fortunately he changed the subject and asked her about her visit to Europe.

80

"Is London the only city you have seen?"

"I was staying with a friend, but if I hadn't taken this job I would have visited Paris and Rome before going back to the States."

"Not Madrid?" he asked teasingly.

"I had not thought of it," she confessed. "I wished to see Nôtre Dame and Sacré Coeur, and the Roman churches, naturally. I did a course, for interest, on Church architecture, and I have seen so many photographs and paintings of them that I wanted to see them for myself."

"You would like the cathedral in Palma then. When Gene can spare you for a whole day I will take you across in my boat. The best view of it is from the sea, it dominates the harbour and is surrounded by palms."

He appeared to take her acceptance for granted and Pippa wondered why he was willing to spend so much time on his uncle's secretary when there were other far more glamorous women clearly anxious for his company. The red haired

81

Liz, who had joined a group of people at the far side of the restaurant, was constantly looking across at them and the bored one had, while the dancing was taking place, again changed the position of her chair and was now facing them, glancing frequently towards Juan.

He ignored both of them and paid Pippa undivided attention, the perfect host. The guitar player had finished and been replaced by a trio, the small space in front of the stage was occupied by a few couples dancing to their rhythmic music, and soon Juan stood up and held out his hand to Pippa.

"Let us dance," he said, giving her no opportunity to refuse even if she had wanted to.

At first he held her impersonally, although she was stiff and nervous at the close contact. Then the sensuous music infected her and she began to relax, laughing at the low commentary he maintained on the foibles of their fellow dancers. He was a superb dancer, she found, unlike the more strenuous but less skilful partners she had had at college balls, who had little idea of how to guide their companions in synchronised movement.

"That's better," Juan murmured, his mouth close to her ear, and pulled her into a firmer hold. Pippa felt intoxicated with the music and the movement, the almost dreamlike quality of a perfectly managed occasion. When the music stopped and Juan's arm remained about her waist as they returned to their table she thought little of it, only faintly realising that it seemed entirely natural that they should be so linked.

They drank coffee and Juan laughingly persuaded Pippa to sample some of the liqueurs made on the island.

"A legacy of the British, who left a secret recipe for gin in the eighteenth century," he told her. "I will take you to the distillery in Mahon, where you can sample as many varieties as you wish and come out reeling drunk!"

"I shall not be sober after any more of these," she protested, and then agreed to try just one more.

It was long after midnight before they left and Pippa gladly agreed with Juan's suggestion that they walked beside the harbour for a while.

"Minorcan roads are far from crowded but there are many sharp bends down to the bay. I have no desire to drive into the sea," he joked, and Pippa looked at him curiously. She was feeling a little light headed as a result of the wine and music but he did not seem affected.

They walked along the edge of the long narrow bay which was the port of Cuidadela, where lights still showed on several boats and in some of the small cafes set in the cliffside, from where laughter and music could still be heard.

Pippa suddenly shivered and Juan drew her closer, his arm about her shoulders.

"Let's go back to the car. I should have suggested that you brought a shawl," he said solicitously, and they turned back to where he had left the car a short distance away. Once inside Pippa was soon warm again and she sat relaxed, dreamy and half asleep as he drove back to the Casa Blanca.

She came to with a gasp of delight as the car rounded one of the last bends leading towards the bay.

"The moon! How beautiful the water

looks with it shining down," she exclaimed, and Juan stopped the car while they sat looking at the silvery brightness, framed by dark shadows of the encircling headlands.

"It is so quiet and peaceful," Pippa almost whispered, as if afraid to disturb the night.

"On the surface," Juan replied. "Beneath there are all sorts of movement, night creatures prowling, and hidden passions ready to unleash untold joy or misery. But it is late and you have to work tomorrow."

Lightly he drew his finger across the curve of her cheek before turning to restart the car, and Pippa felt a wave of hot response to the affectionate gesture sweep through her. The intensity of it shook and frightened her, she had never before experienced such a turmoil of confusion. Her head bowed to conceal her burning face from him she thankfully escaped when he stopped the car briefly beside the door, saying that he would drive it round to the garages before coming in himself.

She fled up the stairs in the dark, silent

house, and stood inside her bedroom door breathing heavily as she tried to regain her composure. What had happened to her? Was she intoxicated? Had the wines and the Minorcan liqueurs been stronger than she had thought at the time? Her fingers trembled as she tried to unfasten the hooks and eyes of her gown, and she had to sit down on the bed for a few minutes to calm her tense nerves. In the silence, broken only by her loudly beating heart, she heard a door close in the distance and footsteps on the stairs. They passed her room without a pause and another door closed, and then she was able to unfasten her dress and crawl exhausted into bed.

She slept fitfully and rose at the normal time heavy eyed and with a dull throbbing headache. Hastily swallowing some aspirin she pulled on a white sleeveless top and a flowered wraparound skirt, then went hesitantly downstairs, unsure of her reactions when she met Juan again.

Gene was alone in the breakfast room and he smiled towards her.

"You're up early," he greeted her. "I

didn't expect you to be up at the usual time."

"It was not terribly late when we got home," she said easily, pouring herself some black coffee. "And there is work to be done."

"Juan has gone swimming," he remarked, eyeing her keenly, and Pippa kept her glance lowered as she strove to reply as casually as possible.

"Has he? He has more energy than I have."

"Will you not have anything to eat, my dear? Are you feeling tired, or out of sorts?"

"I'm not hungry, thank you. We ate so well last night I don't think I'll want food again for the whole of today!"

"I'll take the pages you've already typed and glance over them. I've put out a couple of notebooks that deal with the same period, so far as I can recall. Could you concentrate on them this morning, my dear?"

"Of course."

"There are some sets of figures, salaries and profits from various films. I pasted the official releases into the books and made some comments with figures I had from elsewhere. If you can match them up as far as possible in two columns it would help me. The instructions are in the manual."

Pippa was struggling to follow these instructions some time later, unable to align the columns, when the door of the study opened.

"Hard at work again?" Juan asked and Pippa started, then looked round. He was leaning against the door post grinning at her in a manner that made her catch her breath. Wearing pale fawn jeans, superbly cut, and a matching silk sweater, his dark lithe good looks hit her with the force of a gale, and she felt as breathless as though she had been struggling against one.

"I can't sort these instructions out," she said jerkily, and her heart began to beat faster as he straightened up from his negligent pose and crossed the room towards her.

"Let me see. What is it you want to do?"

"To display these two columns side by side. I thought I pressed this command key, but whenever I do they all arrange themselves in one long column, not two."

He bent over her, studying the screen, and she smelled the faint fragrance of his aftershave while an errant strand of his hair fell against her ear.

"Show me what you have done," he commanded, and she repeated the instructions she had given the machine while he leant over her, one hand to either side of her as he rested them on the table, his face almost touching hers.

"I cannot think what else to do," she murmured in a constrained voice.

"I have it now. Look, instead of doing all this let's see what happens if we use the other way."

Rapidly he pressed some of the keys and magically the figures on the screen regrouped themselves as she had wanted them. Impulsively she turned towards him.

"How on earth did you manage it? I've been trying for hours!"

Instead of replying he bent his head slowly forwards across the few inches that separated them and gently kissed her on the tip of her nose.

"I've been wanting to do that ever since I first saw you," he breathed, and Pippa suddenly found that his arms, which were still either side of her as she sat on the typing chair, had folded about her and she was being pulled inexorably to her feet.

She closed her eyes momentarily, and then they fluttered open as he clasped her to his hard body, his hands on her waist and shoulders, and his lips met hers in a brief but shattering kiss.

He released her quickly and caught both her hands in his. His eyes were triumphant, laughing, as he looked down at her.

"Come sailing with me after lunch," he said quietly and Pippa, trembling and speechless, stared back at him.

He apparently took her silence as acceptance for he squeezed her hands before releasing her.

"I'll go and get the boat ready. See you later."

He was gone as suddenly as he had come and Pippa walked unsteadily across to an easy chair, sinking into it with a deep sigh. What had happened? In just a few seconds she felt that her whole world had turned upside down and inside out. She was as drained as though she had walked for a whole day through muddy fields, and yet she tingled all over with a new sensation. How could any man have this effect on her?

She tried to recapture the fleeting experience of that devastating kiss but found it impossible. How could such a slight embrace have such a deep effect? None of Frank's kisses, however long or ardent, had ever affected her in this way, and yet the merest touch of Juan's lips against hers had set her on fire.

She remained lost in contemplation until Maria brought in her coffee, and then found it impossible to concentrate on her work. Gene, if he noticed her abstracted air when he came in to go over some already printed pages, said nothing.

At lunch Juan seemed cool and a little aloof, more concerned over some problem to do with one of his business interests than talking to her. He talked with Gene about the probable necessity of flying to Washington and Pippa's heart did odd things, leaping about and then plunging down into some gloomy depths.

She was being ridiculous, she told herself, to allow one brief kiss to affect her in this way. It clearly had meant no more to Juan than shaking hands. He had most likely forgotten all about it by now. The thought was desolation.

"I will be with you in five minutes, Pippa, but I must phone someone first."

Pippa smiled wanly and went to change into jeans and a tee-shirt. Remembering that it could be cold on the water she found a bright scarlet sweater, telling herself defiantly that the vivid colour would lift her spirits.

Twenty minutes later she was sitting on the patio, her shoulders drooping, wondering if Juan had forgotten her or whether his business problem was going to mean the cancellation of their sail.

It was only by an intense effort of will that she forced herself to remain seated when she would have liked to pace up and down the patio to calm her tumultuous thoughts. She was sitting with closed eyes, furiously concentrating on repeating to herself all the lines she could recall of 'Hiawatha', when she started to her feet as an arm was placed lightly across her shoulder.

"I cannot apologise enough, Pippa," Juan said. "I could have wished my wretched manager at the bottom of the sea while he rambled on about stupid little problems he could have been solving himself. Do you forgive me for keeping you waiting?"

"Of course," Pippa replied, and the effort of trying to speak normally made her sound curt instead.

"Come, let us waste no more time."

He took her hand and started to run through the gardens down to the beach. Suddenly light hearted, Pippa kept pace with him, arriving laughing and breathless at the small jetty where his boat, a sleek, white and green painted catamaran, rested.

Swiftly Juan helped Pippa into the boat, set the sails and cast off. There was only a slight breeze but enough to fill the sails and take them out of the bay, where Pippa found that a whole series of grey rocky headlands stretched on either hand.

They sailed south for some time away from the land, and Pippa caught glimpses of hotels set amongst trees at the few resorts visible in this corner of the island. A few villas perched on the tops of the cliffs and to the west the tower of the Cape d'Artruch lighthouse was just discernible in the slight haze.

Juan was clearly an expert sailor and Pippa sat dreamily, content to watch him as he talked about the coastline, the many raids that had taken place during earlier times, and the numerous ancient remains to be found all over the island.

"Are you interested in archeological finds?" he asked, and Pippa suddenly thought of the man she had sat beside in the plane, David Nightingale. Only a few days since, it seemed a lifetime ago and she had barely given him a thought.

"I went to see Stonehenge while I was in England. I cannot imagine how primitive people without tools raised the cross stones."

"We have similar monuments in Minorca but they are in the form of a letter T, with a single upright and a stone balanced on top. They are called taulas, they occur only here and no-one knows the purpose of them. Shall we go and see some? There are several good examples."

"I would like that."

He seemed to have given up the idea of going to the States, Pippa thought, her spirits rising magically, and she chatted eagerly of the places she had visited in England while Juan steered the boat towards a small cove slightly to the west of Gene's house.

There was a flat rock to one side of the small beach at just the right height out of the water to form a natural jetty, and even an outjutting spur to provide somewhere to tie the rope.

"This beach is completely inaccessible from the land, except possibly to mountaineers," Juan explained. "A perfect place for a picnic. Maria packed some food for me this morning."

He helped Pippa scramble out onto the rock and handed up to her a small wicker basket. She carried it along the rocks to the sand and he followed with a huge beach towel which he spread out in the centre of the small cove.

"Shall we swim first?" he asked, and as Pippa nodded he quickly slipped off his jeans and shirt, under which he was wearing a brief pair of black swimming trunks. Pippa, who had put on a bright green bikini when she changed after lunch, also took off her upper clothes and Juan grinned boyishly.

"Race you to the rocks over there," he challenged, and they ran splashing into the water and struck out for the rocks at the far side of the bay from the landing place, where some flat rocks sloped down into the sea.

Juan reached them first and scrambled out. Pippa shivered, but not at the water temperature, for today it was much warmer. His slim body had not an ounce of spare flesh, yet his shoulders were broad, and his muscles demonstrated that he was in perfect condition. His hair was partially covering his face and he shook it back out of his eyes and sat on the rocks, leaning back on one elbow as he watched Pippa swim the last few yards.

"Come up here," he said lazily and she climbed up beside him. The rocks were warm and smooth and Juan lay back, his head pillowed on his arms. "Why should a girl like you wish to bury herself on a small, peaceful island?" he asked softly. "What are the men in California and London like that they permit it?"

"I — wanted to prove to my father that I could get a job on my own and support myself," Pippa replied slowly.

"And the young man who was annoying you in the hotel? Had he anything to do with this decision?"

"He — his father is my father's partner. Frank is going to join the firm when he has completed the course he is doing in London. He — was trying to persuade me not to take the job," Pippa explained hastily.

"A cautious man," Juan said, reaching out and taking Pippa's hand in his. A tremor ran through her as he linked his fingers with hers. "Did he hope to marry you?"

"Our fathers wanted it," Pippa admitted.

"And you did not. Wise child. He was not right for you. He could not love you as you were intended to be loved."

He smiled, staring into her eyes, and Pippa could not look away. Just as she thought she would lose her senses he suddenly sat up, leaned across and took her face between both of his hands.

"You must make no hasty choices, little Pippa. Think well before you commit yourself. Now, let us see what Maria has packed for us."

Before Pippa could reply he had dived cleanly into the water and was pulling towards the beach with long, powerful strokes. By the time she had followed he was laying out on the towel some cold legs of chickens, hard boiled eggs, and huge fleshy tomatoes. He was opening a bottle of wine and poured out a tumblerful which he handed to Pippa.

"To your happiness," he said and poured another glass, holding it up to the light before drinking deeply.

When they had finished the salad he unwrapped some of Maria's special fruit cake, a spicy, sticky confection, and carefully divided it into two.

"I shall not be able to eat dinner," Pippa said with a laugh, but as she had already discovered the excellence of the cake she willingly took the slice he offered her.

"My parents died when I was ten," he said abruptly. "I spent a great deal of time with Gene during school holidays and Maria always made me this cake. If she had not been in California most of the time, I swear I would have run away from school on more than one occasion simply to gorge myself on this cake."

Pippa felt a pang of sorrow. Poor little boy, she thought tenderly. Maria must have mothered him, too, as well as providing culinary delights. She swallowed the last few crumbs and grimaced at her sticky fingers. Then Juan reached across and took her hand in his.

He lifted Pippa's hands towards his mouth and gently ran his tongue across them. The quiver of ecstasy shot up her arm and suffused all over her body in a tingling glow. Slowly, savouring every moment, Juan kissed the palms of her hands and when he drew her towards him she went unresisting.

For an agonisingly long minute he held her by the shoulders, his face a few inches from hers, and looked deep into her eyes. She stared back as though mesmerised, her lips parted slightly, breath suspended, and then exhaled as he slid his hands across her back and touched her lips with his own.

His kiss was brief and gentle, his lips playing over hers without force or violence, but Pippa understood the controlled passion behind it and responded as she had never done to the breathless, fierce embraces Frank or some of her other dates had pressed upon her. She felt as though fires had been lit inside her and her head was full of shooting stars, while time and the external world ceased to matter. Nothing of importance existed beyond this small Spanish cove. This, she told herself with a feeling of exhilaration such as she had never before experienced, must be love.

5

THE remainder of the time spent in the cove was devoted to talking about Pippa's life in California, Juan's estates in Spain and his American business, and comparing notes about the places both had visited in England. Apart from mentioning that he had been educated in England Juan spoke little of his childhood, and recalling his reference to the loss of his parents Pippa guessed that the topic was painful for him.

"We should be starting back," Juan said at last, beginning to collect together the remains of their picnic. Pippa gathered the glasses and wrapped them in a napkin, then as she went to place them in the basket her hands touched Juan's. He took them in his and suddenly, with a suppressed murmur, pulled her tightly into his arms, and it was some time later before they could tear themselves apart and reluctantly begin the short journey back to Casa Blanca.

The wind was against them and they moored the catamaran in the bay with only just enough time to change quickly for dinner. Pippa chose a softly pleated dress in a misty grey-blue colour, white shoes and a rope of blue and white beads which she twisted into a knot while she went down the stairs.

Juan was already there, impeccably dressed as he always was in the evenings in formal dinner suit and an exquisitely embroidered dress shirt. He poured the sherry and brought it across to her immediately, smiling intimately as he looked deep into her eyes. He opened his mouth to speak, but at that moment the door opened and Gene came in.

"Oh, Juan, there was a message from Meissen. It sounded urgent and he asked particularly if you could ring him tonight."

Juan nodded. "The Brazilian contract, I suppose. There was a hitch delaying signing. I'll arrange a call now for after dinner, if you'll excuse me."

Dinner was announced when he returned, and afterwards he was closeted in his room dealing with his call, only rejoining Pippa and Gene as the latter was saying goodnight.

"Was it settled?" Gene asked.

"I think so but he wants to keep in touch. Pippa, if he rings early tomorrow and I can get away, shall we go and explore some of those taulas tomorrow afternoon?"

"I'd love to if Gene can spare me."

"You're doing well, my dear, and you did work at the weekend as soon as you arrived. Of course I can spare you. Now I'll say goodnight."

He smiled at them both and went out and Juan crossed the room to Pippa. Placing his hands on either side of her face he drew her towards him and slowly, lingeringly, kissed her lips.

"Sleep well, little one."

Good advice, but impossible to obey, Pippa thought some time later as she lay wide awake in bed, counting the stars she could see through her open window. Her body still thrilled from Juan's kisses, and she was too deliriously happy in her newly discovered love to want to embrace the forgetfulness of sleep.

Even when sleep eventually came it

was shot through with dreams of Juan, his tanned lithe body, his thin but strong hands, so firm and yet when they held her so gentle.

Juan had almost finished breakfast when Pippa, wearing jeans and a loose blouson top in pale blue cotton, sprigged with tiny white sprays of flowers, entered the breakfast room. He smiled across at her, his eyes crinkling and his lips forming the faintest suggestion of a kiss before he turned back to reply to a question Gene had asked.

"No, I don't think so, they can manage perfectly well without me."

"Good. Pippa, my dear, I have some old friends coming for dinner tonight. They're staying at Mahon for a few days in their yacht. Juan suggests that after he has shown you the Torre d'en Gaumés this afternoon you both go into Mahon to fetch my friends."

"We shall already be at the eastern end of the island, and I can show Pippa some of the new developments as well as bronze age villages," Juan said. "If you agree, that is?" he turned politely to Pippa.

"Of course, I'd love to go. I saw nothing of Mahon coming here since the airport is well out of the town."

"Then if you'll excuse me, Pippa, I've letters to write this morning."

"That reminds me," Gene said as Juan strolled out of the room, "I was feeling energetic yesterday afternoon and so I dictated a few letters. They're on the tape already in the machine. I'd be grateful if you could do them for me this morning, Pippa."

"Of course. Did I set out the accounts as you wanted them yesterday? Juan helped me to find the right keys," she added quickly, burying her face in the coffee cup to hide her tell-tale blush as she recalled the kiss he had given her then.

"I haven't looked at them yet. I'll do that while you do the letters, and then we'll go over them."

The letters were brief and unimportant. It seemed as though Gene had been clearing up a variety of uninteresting items of correspondence, and Pippa soon had a small pile of typed letters awaiting his signature. She had just switched on the tape recorder for the next one when Maria brought in her coffee.

"It's a lovely day again, miss," Maria said as she put the tray on a small table.

"It always seems lovely here," Pippa replied.

"Oh, there can be storms, and the wind is strong at times," Maria shrugged. "Mr Watson said please to excuse him but he wishes to finish something before he joins you, he is having coffee in the drawing room."

Pippa nodded and poured herself a cup of the fragrant beverage. Then she looked round, startled, as the sound of a piano came to her. So far as she knew, there was none in the house.

After a moment a woman's voice, speaking in Spanish, came to her and then a short burst of orchestral music. Pippa laughed in relief and went to switch off the tape recorder. Clearly it had been left running in the same way as she had forgotten it and had picked up part of a radio programme. While she had her coffee she went quickly through the rest of the tape to ensure

106

that there were no more letters dictated, but it was obvious that Gene had merely forgotten to switch it off. He seemed to have turned on the radio for a while, then Luis came in to remind him that it was time to change for dinner, and then silence until the tape finished.

Some time later, as Pippa was transcribing another tape of Gene's early reminiscences, he came into the room.

"These are fine, just as I wanted them. Have you enough to do? I want to go into Cuidadela with Luis before lunch."

"Would you like to take in your letters? I've finished them."

"Oh, yes, I can read them in the car. Will you ring this number for me in London and ask the manager to send me this list of books as soon as possible. I need them for references, I've decided."

Pippa took the list and as Gene disappeared through the door she moved to pick up the telephone receiver.

" — how boring it is here at Formentor!" a woman's voice said peevishly.

"It's not for much longer, Sally-Jayne," Juan replied, and Pippa was so startled that she stood holding the receiver to her ear. Why was Juan telephoning Gene's ex-wife, she wondered.

"Too long!" Sally-Jayne replied. "Surely you can hurry things up, darling!"

"Leave the details to me, that's my job and I'll — " Pippa heard before she hastily replaced the receiver on its rest, becoming guiltily conscious that she was listening to a private conversation. Juan had a telephone extension in his room and must have telephoned Sally-Jayne from there. It could not have been Sally-Jayne calling him because Pippa would have heard the bell ringing.

Formentor, that was on Majorca, Pippa suddenly thought, and went to look at a small map of the Balearic Islands hanging on the wall. Yes, Cape Formentor, the northerly spike on the larger island, pointing towards Minorca and one of the nearest places to it. She recollected hearing that there was also an hotel of the same name, a rather exclusive hotel with private beaches and large grounds, just the sort of hotel Sally-Jayne would stay in.

So she was still in Majorca and Juan

for some reason was in touch with her. It's none of my business, Pippa told herself angrily, and went back to typing Gene's account of his first marriage when he had been very young and just beginning to get known in Hollywood.

She remembered to put through the call an hour later just before lunch, and as she finished Luis came in to tell her that the meal was served.

Juan seemed preoccupied, making mechanical conversation, but he threw off his abstraction when they were drinking coffee on the patio, and began to explain to Pippa the various prehistoric remains to be seen on the island.

"There are three talayots in the Torre d'en Gaumés, which is a small settlement on high ground. The talayots are towers, but no-one is certain what they were used for. They might have been look-out towers, or storehouses, but not all of them have inner rooms. There are no others known anywhere else in the world."

"Were they burial chambers?" Pippa asked, intrigued.

"No human remains have ever been

found near them so it is unlikely. Have you finished coffee? Then let's be off and Gene can go and rest."

Soon they were driving towards Mahon. Juan pointed out places of interest as they went, and Pippa, the breeze ruffling her curls as the powerful open-topped car ran smoothly along, studied Juan's face.

His profile was clear cut and incredibly handsome, she told herself for the hundredth time. She had been typing accounts of some of the romantic roles Gene had played in his youth, and although Gene had been and still was handsome, Pippa considered that Juan would have been an irresistible heart throb if he had been a film actor.

"We must visit the Sanctuary at Mount Toro one day. There is a magnificent view from the top. But not today. I'm going south from Alayor."

He drove through narrow twisting lanes for a while, and then along a straight road which ended near a farmhouse at a gateway in a stone wall.

"Here we are, I'll park just inside."

Pippa looked round her in surprise.

"Is this the village?"

She could see little apart from grassy mounds within the encircling walls, and a small ancient car parked close to what looked like a heap of stones a farmer had piled up after clearing his fields.

"What did you expect?" Juan asked, amused.

"Is there no guide, no kiosk to pay entrance fees?"

"There are not enough visitors to make it worth while. Come, we can drive round, there is a decent road, but it's better to walk."

He took Pippa's hand as they set off along the road, and she began to realise that the heaps of stones were in fact small circular rooms, and the larger talayots came into view further round the site.

"Couldn't they have been burial chambers?" Pippa asked.

"There were navetas which seemed to be tombs. The name comes from the shape, like an overturned boat. We can see one near Cuidadela which is in good condition."

They walked on, and round a corner as the road dropped sharply they came across the driver of the other car who was busy taking pictures of the talayot. He looked up as he heard their voices and exclaimed in surprise.

"Hi there! Remember me? David Nightingale."

Pippa smiled, pleased to have met the young man from the plane again.

"Hello. I met David on the plane to Mahon," she explained. "This is Conte Juan y Correa, David, my employer's nephew."

The men shook hands and although Juan appeared to be perfectly friendly, Pippa sensed a reserve in his manner as he talked to David, asking him about his work.

"How long do you plan to stay here?" he asked eventually.

"Another month or so, I think, and then I'll move on to Majorca. Look me up sometime, Pippa, you know where I'm staying."

He looked at Juan as he spoke, but if he hoped for an invitation he was disappointed. Juan remained silent and Pippa could hardly issue an invitation on her own.

"I may do so," she answered, a little

embarrassed, and was thankful when Juan said that they had to be leaving.

As they drove away Juan was quiet, his firm chin jutting out and a slight crease between his eyes. Pippa longed to clasp his hand and reassure him that David Nightingale meant nothing to her, he was a mere acquaintance and she would not mind if she never saw him again, but she dared not. It would seem like taking liberties, and she could not yet accustom herself to behaving towards Juan as she would have done, a few weeks ago, to Frank.

"After the old, the new," Juan said suddenly, turning to smile warmly at her. They had been heading eastwards again, along a road near to the coast, and he turned off now towards the sea.

"New? You mean new buildings?" Pippa asked. "But there must be hundreds of them all over the island since the tourists came."

"Not like Binibeca. We're here, we'll park at the top."

He led her down a steep slope towards a tiny bay. On their left were many houses, crammed together in haphazard style with alleys leading into courtyards and through to the road above and behind the houses.

"How do you like our new old-world fishing village?" Juan asked as they reached the small beach and turned to gaze at the row of houses running out along one side of the bay.

"You mean it is all new?" Pippa exclaimed. "I thought that it had just been painted and tidied up!"

"It makes a pleasant change from the rash of holiday chalets and new town developments everywhere else," Juan said with a grin. "The houses are at different levels, and have a variety of ornamental Spanish and Moorish decorations, but it is a little like Hollywood's attempt to build a medieval castle."

They drove slowly along the coast past some of the other types of new housing, and Pippa sighed for the lost landscape which was no longer flat and empty as it fell gradually to the sea, but scarred with new roads and brash new bungalows.

They went through Villa Carlos and Juan explained that the old name had been Georgetown.

"In honour of George the Third. The British built it in the 1770s and the architecture is typically eighteenth century English, like that house with flat sash windows and a door with brass knocker and lamps, and a half moon fanlight. Mahon is more Spanish, but if we're to pick up Gene's friends we haven't time to explore today."

He drove through the town straight to the quayside, and they soon found the yacht 'Charleston', and Pippa was introduced to John and Peggy Finlay, a middle aged couple who had known Gene's family since he and Gene had been at high school together.

"We always spend several months cruising in the Med and usually visit Gene a couple of times each year," Peggy explained once she had discovered exactly what Pippa's position in the household was. "I'm glad he's started his memoirs at last, he's been talking about them for long enough. It will give him something to think about. How far has he got, my dear?"

"We're still sorting out all the notebooks and tapes, I'm typing them," Pippa explained, but almost before she had finished Peggy was talking again.

"I guess it'll take him years. Do you remember the time he wanted to write a film script, John? It took him two years just to plot out the idea."

She went on talking but Pippa stopped listening. So the Finlays did not know that Gene had only a short time to live. She realised that Gene had never mentioned that fact to her. She had overheard it during the quarrel with Sally-Jayne. Most likely he preferred people in general not to know. He would hate their sympathy and the feeling that they were watching him for signs of failing powers.

Peggy maintained a virtual monologue during the drive to Casa Blanca. Her husband contributed the occasional "Yes, dear," and Juan interjected remarks every so often, but Pippa answered only when Peggy, in the manner of one distributing favours evenly amongst her companions, spoke directly to her.

Sitting back in the corner of the back seat Pippa studied the Finlays. He was big, broad shouldered and with a decided paunch. His hair receded and the wisps that remained were a pale grey colour, contrasting with the red weatherbeaten complexion. From one of Peggy's remarks Pippa deduced that he had made a fortune as an exporter, but quite what he had exported remained obscure. It had been, however, to the Mediterranean countries. Although now retired from active business, with three sons carrying it on, he liked to keep in contact with his former territory.

Peggy herself could have been twenty or thirty years younger than John, with carefully bleached and sculptured hair, a still good clear skin, and a trim, well controlled figure. Although she talked endlessly she made no unpleasant remarks about mutual acquaintances, even when she referred to Sally-Jayne.

"We ran into her in Palma," she explained. "Does Gene know she is here?"

"She has been to the Casa Blanca," Juan said shortly.

"Really? She didn't say that but perhaps she hadn't been then. Such a pity she couldn't have stayed with

Gene, he's been so unfortunate with both Mary and Louise dying. Yet there didn't seem to be another man around. She's so lovely I'd have expected her to have married again before now."

"Here we are, Peggy," Juan said with a faint note of relief in his voice as he halted the car before the door. Luis appeared at once and the Finlays greeted him as an old friend.

"Mr Watson is on the patio. If you would like to come straight through I will take up the cases later."

They disappeared and Pippa ran up to her room to change for dinner. She was pondering Peggy's remark about Gene's wives dying, and wondering what had happened. She had not reached this part of his story yet although that morning she had typed several references to his first wife, Mary, and had realised then that he had been very much in love with her, marrying her within a week of being sent home slightly wounded in the last few months of the Second World War.

She banished fruitless speculations from her mind and wondered what to wear, finally choosing the blue silk dress, demurely high at the neck and with long, close fitting sleeves. She fastened a pair of silver chains about her neck and clasped a silver charm bracelet on her wrist. Then, judging that the Finlays had been given enough time to greet Gene and unpack, she went downstairs.

Juan was waiting on the patio and he smiled appreciatively as she went out to join him.

"Pretty, dainty little Pippa," he said lightly. "Gene will be back in a moment, but have your sherry now."

Pippa sat in one of the white painted chairs. It was warm and still. The wind which blew for much of the time had dropped and it was warmer than she had yet known it so late in the day.

She sipped her sherry, looking at Juan who was standing at the edge of the patio gazing silently out across the bay. It seemed incredible to her at that moment that he had ever kissed her, and she shivered suddenly. She might love him but why should someone so handsome and rich and eminently attractive feel more for her than a mild liking? She was here and had made it plain that she was willing, indeed anxious for his attentions. No doubt he regarded her as a pleasant diversion while he remained with his uncle.

These thoughts fled later, however, when Juan suggested that they stroll in the garden, leaving Gene to chat with his old friends over brandies.

As soon as they were out of sight of the uncurtained windows he slipped his arm round her waist and pulled her close, dropping a featherlight kiss on her hair. Companionably linked they strolled on to the end of the path where a stile built into the stone wall gave access to the uncultivated, scrub covered hillside.

"Shall we walk up to the headland this way?" he asked. "There is quite a good path, you won't twist your ankle or ruin your shoes."

"It doesn't look far, yes, let's go."

He led the way, holding one hand while Pippa held her skirts away from the stone with the other. As she reached the top he was below her on the other side, and swiftly seized her by the waist and swung her effortlessly down, then pulled her close into his arms.

"Do you realise how tempting, how delectable you are in that prim little dress?" he murmured softly as he nibbled gently at her ear. A shiver of delight ran down Pippa's back and she clung to him shamelessly, responding eagerly when, after a tantalisingly long time while he explored her neck and cheeks with soft yet insistent lips, he brought his mouth hard down on hers.

Suddenly he released her.

"Come, we'll never reach the headland like this," he said huskily and took her hand in his, beginning to walk on. Stumbling slightly Pippa followed, dazed, happy, and content in the knowledge that he still found her attractive. It no longer mattered when they were so close, hand in hand and isolated on the hillside, whether she was a mere diversion to him or something more. For the moment all that mattered was that they were together, and that every few yards he stopped to kiss her, so that it was fully dark and late and the others had all gone to bed when they finally returned to the house.

6

PIPPA woke early on the following morning and lay in bed recalling the delights of the walk the previous evening. Then, restless and energetic, she decided to swim in the pool before breakfast. Covering her brief black bikini with a towelling robe she went downstairs. Noises from the kitchen showed that Maria was already working but there was silence elsewhere.

After several lengths at top speed, Pippa clambered out of the pool and stood looking across the bay while she towelled her hair dry. In the distance a powerful speedboat was heading westwards, but she could not tell whether it had come from their bay or further along the coast. A moment later it had disappeared behind the cliffs and she turned to go indoors. Maria was carrying a tray of used dishes back into the kitchen.

"Good morning, Miss. You are up early. Did you enjoy your swim?"

"Yes, thank you, Maria, and ready for a huge breakfast!"

Maria laughed. "It will be ready in ten minutes."

It was going to be another hot day, so Pippa found a loose cheesecloth dress and flat thonged sandals. She would swim again later, she decided, and hoped that Juan might suggest another visit to the cove. Eager to see him again she ran downstairs but Gene was alone in the breakfast room.

"I'm going to Cuidadela this morning with Peggy and John," he said when she sat down opposite him. "Some distant relatives, a cousin's son I think, is at the American communication base and lives there. They want to call on him. Have you plenty of work?"

"Yes, there are still lots of tapes," Pippa answered, and since Juan did not appear she soon excused herself and went to begin them.

A short while later she heard the car leaving and then all was silent until Maria brought her coffee.

"I'll have it outside, I think, Maria, it's so hot."

She sat on the patio but there was no sign of Juan. With Gene and Luis gone the house was eerily silent. When she had finished her coffee she strolled along to the end of the house and stood there for a moment. A quick glance had shown her that the Mercedes was still in the garages, so where could Juan be? She did not care to ask. Disappointed, she went back to her work. He would be there at lunch.

The tape she was now doing gave her one answer to some of the questions she had asked herself the previous night. Mary, Gene's first wife, had shared in some of his early successes but had given up a promising career when she had become pregnant. She had lost three babies with early miscarriages and then, despite the warnings of the doctors, tried yet again, spending almost the whole of her pregnancy in bed.

"It was my fault because she knew how much I wanted a son," Gene's voice had said, still full of emotion after all these years. "I let her persuade me that with great care she might carry the child. I let her dismiss the dangers, thinking that they only referred to the probability of

124

another miscarriage, which would have been dreadful enough but nothing like the horror of losing my darling."

Mary had given birth a few weeks before term, but the child had been stillborn and Mary herself feverishly ill. Distraught with sorrow she had appeared to make no effort to recover her strength, and a month afterwards had succumbed to an infection and died.

After weeks of self hatred and despair, during which he had disappeared and been found eventually living rough in the mountains, Gene had thrown himself into his work. These next few years had been his most successful. Never short of work he had obtained increasingly important roles and was predicted as one of the future great stars.

Pippa was dealing with some of the many studio rows when she heard the car return, and soon afterwards Luis announced that lunch was ready on the patio.

They were seated at a small table under a couple of huge gaily striped umbrellas. There were only four places laid.

"Where's Juan?" she asked before she could stop herself.

"He'll be back in a few days," Gene said easily. "I think it must have been connected with a phone call which came late last night. He took the boat so I take it he's gone to Majorca. There are more flights from there if he has to go to Madrid, but he may have gone to London or Paris, he didn't say."

And he'd left her no message, Pippa thought bleakly. That must have been his boat which she had seen after her morning swim. He might have written her a brief note, if only to say that he would soon be back. When Peggy announced that she and John were going to adopt the siesta habit and Gene disappeared into his own room, Pippa went back to the study and tried to distract her thoughts from Juan by typing until her head was swimming.

She went out and walked along the same path they had taken the previous night, stopping at each spot where Juan had taken her into his arms and trying to relive the kisses and embraces they had shared. But it did no good, the elation and joy she had experienced then had vanished and all she could think of was the fact that he had not bothered to tell her that he was going away or when he would return.

Somehow she maintained a cheerful expression that evening, smiling and responding to Peggy's remarks. She was thankful for the older woman's garrulity which enabled her to remain quieter than usual, and soon after they had moved to the drawing room she tactfully excused herself, saying that she ought to write some letters home.

Finding that she could not read, the words of her novel dancing about before her eyes as she constantly thought of Juan and his apparent desertion of her, without explanation, she did try to write letters. One to her parents, briefly describing her job and trying to reassure them that she was coping excellently on her own, was soon completed. She contemplated sending one to Frank but in the end wrote a friendly message on a postcard, wishing him well and giving no hope of any future reconciliation. Then she settled down to a long letter to Dolores, describing all she had seen. Although she tried to conceal her feelings for Juan as much as possible his name inevitably cropped up several times in her letter, and she almost tore the pages across. In the end however, she sealed the envelope. Dolores might tell Frank that she appeared to have met a new man and it would be easier than telling him herself, especially as she had nothing to tell apart from the fact that Juan had kissed her several times and she was in love with him.

Eventually she undressed and went to bed, but sleep was elusive. She dozed until dawn and then fell into a deep sleep, waking only when Maria came in to see whether she was all right.

"The others have finished breakfast and gone out in the boat," she explained as Pippa opened weary eyes.

"Oh, dear, what will Mr Watson think of me?" Pippa exclaimed.

"He said you had worked very hard yesterday, more than you should have done, and you were to rest. Shall I bring your breakfast up here?"

"No, of course not, Maria. I'll be down in a few minutes."

"It's no bother."

"But with guests in the house you have far more than usual to do. I'll be down soon."

Feeling depressed and exhausted, Pippa had a cool shower and splashed her face with cold water. Feeling much refreshed, but still carrying a heavy weight over her heart she went downstairs. After breakfast she again worked hard at the tapes, but she was so tired that she willingly agreed with Gene's concerned suggestion at lunch that she took a siesta.

"You have been working too hard," he told her chidingly. "We are all going out tonight to dinner, you too if you will, and I don't want you to be too tired."

She slept heavily, waking still unrefreshed. A quick swim in the sea helped a little, and then she dressed in the same frock she had worn when Juan had taken her out to dinner.

They went to a small roadside restaurant on the new road to the Cala Santa Galdana, which Gene said had a growing reputation.

"We stayed at the Cala Santa Galdana once," Peggy said. "It's a beautiful cove,

129

one of the loveliest on Minorca apart from the small private ones like your own, Gene. But who was Saint Galdana?"

"There isn't one. The region used to be called after Santa Ana, then the Arabs called it Guad-al-Ana, and after the Spanish reconquered the island in the thirteenth century they put Santa before the Arab name and it became Santa Galdana."

"Pity, Galdana would make a pretty name for a girl," Peggy commented and went on to discuss her favourite names, bemoaning the fact that she had never had a daughter. Pippa's attention wandered as she thought of David Nightingale, who was staying in the village. She must take up Gene's offer and borrow the small car Luis used when he went shopping and perhaps she would visit David, or at least go and see the bay which was supposed to be so beautiful.

Somehow that idea was not very attractive. David was a pleasant enough man, from what little she had seen of him, but he wasn't Juan! Yet she was being foolish to spend her time thinking of Juan. How could he possibly find it anything more than a pleasant flirtation with herself? She was fairly pretty, she thought without vanity, but Juan must be able, with his looks and wealth, to attract the most ravishing of creatures. She was insignificant while he could have anyone he wanted. Probably he was laughing at her for the easy way she had fallen into his arms.

He had not always paid her compliments. Her face burned as she recalled their first few meetings. He had been sarcastic on the first occasion, finding her preening herself before the mirror, and angry later. It was only when she had been living in the same house that he had been pleasant towards her. That might have been because he considered it his duty as her employer's nephew, or because it would be awkward to have remained cool.

But that did not make it necessary for him to spend time taking her out, or force him to kiss her, she protested silently. He was probably bored, and flirting with her, seeing how easily his charm enslaved her, was a mere amusement. If it had been more surely he would have mentioned that he was going away.

She recalled that sudden late night call. He could not have told her himself, and possibly it would have seemed too pointed to leave her a note. The thought cheered her momentarily. Perhaps he did care for her a little. He might not want to draw attention to their relationship before it was more definite.

Yet would it become more definite? Pippa realised suddenly that despite his kisses and compliments Juan had never breathed a word of love, or made the slightest reference to a future together. Her spirits plummeted again and she had difficulty in responding adequately to the others.

Fortunately Gene kept early hours and they soon left to drive home. Pippa went straight to bed, and so exhausted was she by the turmoil of her emotions that she fell into a deep sleep.

She worked hard on the following day, Friday, and still there was no word of Juan. It was hard to believe that she had been in Minorca for just a week, so much had happened. In the afternoon, when she was resting on a lounger chair on her bedroom balcony, Maria brought her a letter from England.

"You are not forgotten," she said with a smile. "Dinner will be early this evening, Luis is driving Mr and Mrs Finlay back to their yacht afterwards."

"I hadn't realised that they were going so soon."

"They will return in a week or so. Mr Finlay does not care to leave it in the charge of his crew for too long at a time. He says they get slack. I think he enjoys returning unexpectedly to try to catch them out," Maria said with a sniff.

On Saturday Gene tried to persuade Pippa to have the day off.

"You've been hard at it the last few days and should not work at the weekends in any case," he said when he came into the study and found her typing.

"I am quite happy doing it, I find it interesting," she replied truthfully, but she did not say that she needed to keep herself occupied to prevent herself from brooding about Juan.

"Well, if you really want to. I must get down to reading it all or I'll never catch up with you," Gene said with a laugh. "I have done nothing with the Finlays here. They said how lucky I was to have found you," he added, and rested his hand on her head. "I know it too, my dear, there are very few like you."

She turned slightly to smile up at him as he stood beside her, and then they both turned as the door to the study closed sharply. They had not heard it open.

Juan stood with his back to the door, observing them with a slightly sardonic gleam in his eyes.

"Do you never give Pippa some time off, Gene?" he asked lightly.

Pippa tried desperately to hide the delight she felt at seeing him so unexpectedly, while Gene laughed ruefully.

"I've just been trying to persuade her to relax. Perhaps you'll be more successful, Juan."

He moved away to sit at his desk and Juan strolled over to the window. He wore tight fitting white jeans and a dark blue sweater. His hair was wind blown and Pippa realised that he must have just returned on his boat.

"I hope so," he was replying to Gene.

"It's Liz's barbecue tonight, Pippa, I was hoping you'd come with me. I came back early to go to it."

Helplessly she found herself agreeing. She had not really liked the red-haired Liz, but to go anywhere with Juan would be better than the thought of him surrounded by beautiful, predatory females. She realised anew how much she had missed him during these past few days.

Later, in her room, she upbraided herself angrily. He had only to throw out a casual invitation and she leaped to meet it, eager as a puppy chasing a piece of string. Was she tied to him by such a piece of string, she wondered. Why was she so helpless, so utterly without a will of her own? She had not always been so feeble. She had not previously loved a man, she reminded herself. And then she knew that it did not matter whether Juan was secretly laughing at her readiness to jump to his tune. She would make the most of his company, enjoy his attentions while she could for surely soon he would tire of her, and he would have to return to his Spanish estates and his American business some time so she would probably never see him again. She would not think of tomorrow.

She wore loose scarlet pants and a matching top that evening, and found that Juan had abandoned formal evening attire for tight black trousers and a loose, wide sleeved open necked shirt of white embroidered silk. He had a wide emerald green cummerbund tied loosely about his waist and this emphasised his narrow hips and long legs.

The costume made him look especially Spanish, and Pippa thought that he might not have had any non-Spanish blood in him. His even white teeth gleamed in his tanned face, and he looked at the same time unbearably romantic and somehow dangerous. Vague thoughts of the bull ring and the Inquisition flashed through Pippa's mind and were as suddenly banished when he smiled and took her hand in his.

"We'll probably be very late, Gene, Liz's parties have a habit of lasting until dawn."

"I know," Gene said drily. "I used to attend them myself a few years ago.

136

Have a good time, Pippa. And stay in bed all day tomorrow if you feel like it. I've plenty to be going on with to catch up with you."

Juan made no mention of where he had been for the past few days as they drove northwards towards the large house Liz owned on the opposite coast, nor did he explain why he had left so abruptly and not made any effort to tell Pippa when he would return. She carefully avoided all mention of it, paying a great deal of attention to the landscape, which was far more rugged here in the north than in the south of the island.

Liz's house was set on a low cliff, and the grounds sloped at the side towards a small beach. When they arrived they could see a fire already lit on the beach and dozens of people milling round it.

Liz was greeting her guests on a wide terrace which overlooked the beach.

"Hi there, Juan, glad you could make it after all. And Pat, isn't it?"

"Pippa Dawson," Juan corrected. "You always were hopeless with names, Liz. Where's Gerry?"

"On the beach. Darling, do me a

favour, will you? He's being enticed by that little scrub Mandy, and only someone as devastating as you could pry her claws loose. I'll be down soon, but I might scratch her eyes out if I see her hanging on too tightly."

Juan laughed, took two glasses from a tray a waiter offered to him, and led Pippa down a path with wide shallow steps at intervals, leading to the beach.

"Who is Gerry, her husband?" Pippa asked curiously.

"No, von Hauptmann vanished from the scene a year ago. Gerry is the next in line, if she can bring him to the point. I believe she's having some difficulty, he's been married a couple of times before and doesn't see why he should tie himself down again, especially when he can find plenty of admiration without marriage."

He seemed to know everyone there and was clearly very popular, especially with the women. Some of them eyed Pippa curiously while others did their best to detach Juan from her side. To her immense gratitude he refused to be detached, and she began to enjoy the music, the dancing and the feasting.

They ate roast suckling pig, turkeys and steaks, all cooked over the huge fire. Baked potatoes, salads, and gallons of beer and wine and sangria were consumed, and huge baskets of fruit were placed strategically. Some of the guests had brought swim suits and plunged, with cries and shouts, into the cold sea. Most joined in the dancing, enjoying the music of several guitarists who played individually or in groups.

Pippa was sitting on the sand, waiting for Juan to fetch her more wine, when Liz dropped down beside her with a sigh.

"Whew. I'm hot. Where's Don Juan?"

"What did you call him?" Pippa asked in surprise.

"Oh, didn't you know? That's his nickname and I must say it's apt. I've never known a man with so many girl friends as Juan. Is he still seeing Sally-Jayne?"

Pippa gulped and tried to keep her voice from betraying her distress.

"I wouldn't know," she said casually. "He saw her when she came to see Gene, naturally."

And might have been with her in

Majorca these past few days, she added bleakly to herself.

"Is Sally-Jayne still in touch with Gene?" Liz asked, clearly surprised. "I thought she'd set her sights on Juan. After all, he's Gene's heir, and very rich already as well as being younger. A better proposition altogether. And Gene must be a millionaire several times over," she added reflectively. "His family were rich, they still own big engineering firms, and then he didn't waste his money from films as so many stars did, but invested it and made more. And he didn't have to pay alimony to his first two wives, they both died. He only pays Sally-Jayne. She must be praying that he doesn't marry again," she added, giving a crow of laughter.

"Gene, marry again? But — " Pippa said in surprise.

"Oh, he's not too old, and although from all we hear he was the faithful husband, there were lots of girl friends in between marriages. Gene enjoyed women."

Pippa silently admitted that Liz was right. Still handsome, urbane and good company, Gene could well have considered marriage again if it were not for the fact that he had so little time left to him. But, kind and considerate as she had found him to be, she did not think he would ever try to persuade any woman to marry him knowing that he had only a few more months to live.

At that moment Juan returned and Liz rose.

"Be seeing you. Don't keep Pat to yourself all evening, Juan, there are other men who'd like to get to know her," she said over her shoulder as she wandered away.

"Tired?" Juan asked as he stretched full length beside Pippa.

"No-o," she answered slowly. After what Liz had said she would have liked nothing better than to escape, but she had a strong suspicion that Liz wanted her to do something like trying to persuade Juan to leave. She would not give the bitchy redhead that satisfaction, she determined suddenly, even if Liz had been right and Juan was flirting with his uncle's ex-wife.

Defiantly Pippa drank the wine he had brought to her, then demanded that they dance. When another man cut in she went with him willingly, waving to Juan who watched with a crooked smile on his lips and then seized another girl, whirling her into the mêlée.

Gradually the dancing became wilder, more frantic, and Pippa noticed several couples steal away into the shadows of the rocks at the foot of the cliff. She glimpsed Juan dancing close to a small blonde girl, his head bent so close to hers that he might have been kissing her, and flung herself with even greater abandon into the rhythmic swaying, laughing up into her own partner's face as though she had not a care in the world.

At last Juan, with a brief apology to her partner, came back to her. Silently they edged round the other dancers and then he pulled her out of the crush.

"I think we'd best vanish," he said quietly. "I haven't seen Liz for some time so we can't say our farewells."

"I want to stay," she protested, unwilling to let him think that she could be dictated to.

"You had much better not," he said curtly. And then: "You've had more than enough to drink, my dear."

Shocked, Pippa suddenly realised why she was leaning so heavily against him so that he was almost carrying her up the path back to the house.

"I'm not drunk," she protested, horrified.

"No, but you are merry and very tired. I'm taking you home. I've had enough too, as it happens. Liz's parties always get rather out of hand around now."

Pippa nodded. "I can walk on my own," she stated and he released her abruptly. She walked slowly and carefully up the path and did not protest when he slipped his arm about her waist as they walked across the terrace to where he had left the car. Sinking down into the luxurious seat Pippa sighed, leaned her head back, and promptly went to sleep.

She awoke some time later to feel Juan's lips gently caressing hers. Shaking herself she realised hazily that they were still in the car, which Juan had drawn off the road into a narrow track which led into some pine woods.

"My sweet darling," he whispered, a tremble of a laugh in his voice. "Sleeping beauty, but we must talk before we get home."

"I'm sorry, was I asleep? I was not tipsy!" Pippa said vehemently as she recalled the party. Juan laughed.

"No, my lovely little sleepyhead. But it's almost breakfast time and I wanted to ask you something before we got home."

"Mm?" Pippa asked, still not fully awake. "What is it?"

"It's about Gene, I'm worried. You heard that row he had with Sally-Jayne when you first arrived?"

"I couldn't help it," Pippa said slowly, wondering what this was all leading to.

"You heard that Gene's doctors have given him only a few more months to live, a year at most?"

"Yes, I heard that. What is it? Are you telling me that he has even less time?"

"No, no, in fact he might have more if he takes things easily. That is the point. He's working too hard. I want you to give up your job so that he does not feel obliged to work at his memoirs."

"Give up my job?" Pippa exclaimed. "But — you have no right to ask that of me!" she stormed angrily.

"Is it so important to you?"

"Yes, it is! I needed to prove that I could keep myself, to have some self respect! What would happen if I gave it all up after only a week? And I don't believe that it is bad for Gene to work on his memoirs. He is interested and happy!"

"Darling, you don't understand, I want you to come to Spain with me. Pippa, my sweet, it has been such fun showing you this small island. There is so much more in my own country. I must go back soon and I thought that you could come too. Look, if it means so much to you I could provide you with a job too! You could continue to prove your independence to the folk back home and at the same time Gene would have to take it more easily without your support."

"You just want to prevent Gene from publishing his memoirs!" Pippa suddenly blazed at him. "Has Sally-Jayne put you up to this? I think you're despicable, trying to seduce me away from my job just to deprive Gene from his last few pleasures in life. Is that why you've

145

been so attentive? Did you think yourself irresistible? Even if I had left that would not have served. Gene would have got someone else. Had you thought of that? But the extra bother would have made him more worried, caused him to take things less easily! Well, now I know how to value your kisses! I think you're treacherous! And I want to go home!" she finished with a gasp, holding back with a great effort the tears of angry frustration.

"Pippa, my dear," Juan began, but Pippa interrupted him furiously.

"Don't you dare call me your dear! You have used me, tried to make me so pliable to your demands that you think I'd desert Gene just when you whistle! Well you're wrong, I won't! Gene has been good to me, I owe him some loyalty even if you can't feel any. Now will you please take me home or do I have to walk?"

"As you wish," Juan said abruptly, and with an angry gesture turned the ignition key.

He drove home in silence but there was a white line about his mouth, and his eyes were narrowed as he stared rigidly ahead. Beside him Pippa alternated between despair at the sudden ending of all that she had imagined between them, and rage that he had treated her so badly with ulterior motives of preventing his uncle from carrying out his last design.

It must be Sally-Jayne's influence, she thought miserably. He must have been in Majorca with her these last few days. They must have plotted together to try and sabotage Gene's plans, and all the kisses and attentions had been directed towards that end. Pippa squirmed inwardly. What a fool Juan must have thought her. How he and Sally-Jayne must have laughed together as he told her how easily the unsophisticated Pippa had fallen, like a ripe apple, into his arms.

Her cheeks burned with angry humiliation. He had made her believe that she loved him. She blinked back sudden tears. She did love him. An innate honesty forced her to admit that Juan had spoken no word of love. His actions may have given her that impression, but he had said nothing that she could interpret as love rather than flattery. Suddenly she remembered Frank, and she wondered if he had felt the same when she had rejected his love. Why, oh why did life have to be so complicated, she thought despairingly. She ought to hate Juan for what he had done to her, and although she despised him and would for ever be ashamed that she had been so misled, she knew that she still loved him.

They drew up before the door of the Casa Blanca and Juan turned towards her.

"Pippa, my dear, it is not as you think," he began, but she threw off the hand he had placed on her own as if he had stung her, and was already half out of the car.

"I know what to think," she managed, and escaped through the door before her tears could no longer be restrained.

7

WHEN Pippa came down late the following morning Gene told her that Juan had taken out his boat.

"You look tired. A sail would have been good for you," he added, "but Juan was up early."

"I thought I'd like to visit the Gala Santa Galdana," Pippa said, suddenly making up her mind. "May I borrow the car?"

"Of course, any time."

She set off after lunch and dawdled along trying to forget the fury and dismay she felt after last night. How could Juan go behind his uncle's back in so despicable a manner, trying to take away from the older man something he so desperately wanted to do?

She tried not to think how completely she had herself been fooled by Juan's kisses. Of course he felt nothing for her and must think her an utter fool.

She was, she thought angrily, to have imagined for a moment that a man such as Juan would even look at her twice in the normal way.

She tried to take some interest in the scenery but it failed to charm her today. Even the descent into the Gala Santa Galdana, as the broad road swung down past steep cliffs and the almost circular bay appeared on her left, fringed with palms, did nothing to raise her spirits.

She crossed the bridge over the small river and parked the car in front of one of the large hotels, then walked back towards the beach. To both sides the headlands curved protectively, but to her right a small spur of rock protruded into the waters of the bay, and from where she stood Pippa could see through an archway to the headland beyond.

There were children playing with inflatable dingies on the beach to the left, but Pippa craved solitude so she began walking the other way. She discovered some steps leading onto the spur of rock, where there was a small, but at present closed cafe, and she walked through to the further side of what was in effect a short tunnel.

To her disappointment there was no way to reach the river mouth the far side, just a railing at the top of a steep cliff. For some time she stood there, gazing down at the water which was blue and green and brown all at the same time. The cliffs, a pale sandy colour, stretched in thin layers towards the narrow entrance to the bay, topped with a few trees which were permanently bent over by the west winds.

Pippa turned to go and had just emerged from the far side of the tunnel when David appeared in front of her.

"I thought it was you!" he exclaimed triumphantly. "I was on my hotel balcony and saw you park, but by the time I got down to the beach you had disappeared. Are you alone?"

"Yes, I borrowed Gene's car. I've heard so much about this bay," she said hurriedly, not wishing him to think that she had come with the intention of seeking him out.

"It's beautiful," he enthused. "Come and have a drink with me, unless you want to walk through the woods."

"A drink would be fine, thanks. I'm not feeling especially energetic," Pippa replied.

"There's a bar on the road out of the bay, it's not far. Let's cut across the beach."

They walked companionably side by side, and David talked enthusiastically of the work he had already done.

"It is a fantastic place, there are literally hundreds of prehistoric sites, most of them in the middle of fields, humps of stones that the farmers just avoid. What did you think of the Torre d'en Gaumés?"

"I was surprised it was so open, so — lonely," Pippa replied.

"One can't imagine Stonehenge like that," David agreed. "But Avebury, and some of the other sites, are just the same even in England. Will you be going back there when your job here finishes?"

"I don't know. I ought to be thinking of going home then, I suppose. I've been away for six months already since I finished college, and if this job lasts six months my parents will be pressing me to return. They weren't too happy at the idea in the first place and would have stopped me if they could."

He chatted easily, telling her about his own life and his photography, and she responded by relating some stories about her college life. He was surprisingly easy to talk to and the time passed remarkably quickly. When he suggested that she stayed for dinner she agreed readily.

It was a pleasant meal, unexciting but good food and wine, and the only moment of embarrassment was when David mentioned Juan, recalling their previous meeting.

"Did you say he was a Count?" he asked. "Yet I thought your employer was American?"

"His sister, Juan's mother, married a Spaniard," Pippa replied curtly. "Have you ever seen any of Gene's films? I can remember seeing some on television back home but not a great deal about them."

"He played all sorts of parts, cowboys, gangsters, detectives, from what I know. Perhaps he was too versatile to become really great in any one style."

Or made too many powerful enemies with his outspokenness, Pippa thought to herself, recalling some of the rows at the studios Gene had described. But she could not say this and so agreed lightly.

When she regretfully said that she had to go David urged her to see him again, and she agreed to meet him the following day for a boat trip round Mahon harbour.

"It really is fantastic," he enthused, and when she saw it the next afternoon Pippa had to agree. One of the largest harbours in the world, the bay was two and a half miles long and had sheltered many fleets over the centuries.

"This is the leper island," the guide intoned, "and the high walls were built to prevent the infection spreading to Mahon."

Several other islands and shore bases had been garrisoned at various times and Pippa's head was reeling with facts when they returned to the quay.

They wandered up the steep hillside into the old town, through narrow streets and alleyways.

"You must see the covered market," David said as they came out into an open space, and led the way to a busy building beside a large church.

Inside, two wide passageways stretched at right angles, filled with market stalls selling a vast variety of fruit and other goods. David led the way down one of these where small shops opened out in arched alcoves, and at the end turned a corner into a similar passageway.

"Does it remind you of anything?" he asked.

"Does it go round in a square?"

"That's right."

"With a space in the middle — a quadrangle. Could it have been cloisters?" Pippa suddenly asked.

"Yes, attached to a Carmelite convent. A most ingenious conversion, isn't it?"

Pippa admired the high vaulted roof, but could not imagine nuns walking in silent contemplation where now the bustling market operated.

"Any more than I can really see English soldiers controlling the island. I wonder what it was really like in those days?"

"Much more peaceful than now,

despite the fighting which took place occasionally. Shall we have dinner here or go back to my hotel?"

Pippa chose to stay in Mahon and they found a small restaurant overlooking the harbour. Again Pippa found it easy and pleasant, for David was an undemanding companion, well able to keep the conversation going and avoid any awkward pauses when she permitted her thoughts to return to Juan and his perfidious behaviour.

She had left Gene's car in Ferrerias, the town on the main central road near the turning to Cala Santa Galdana, since it had seemed stupid for both of them to drive all the way to Mahon. When David drew up alongside it Pippa made haste to get out of the car, fearing that he would try to kiss her. She felt totally unable to cope with any amorous advances from another man yet, but David moved only to open the door for her. He came to stand by her car door as she got in.

"I enjoyed that, Pippa. Let's meet again soon. I really must work the next few days, but I'll ring you soon if I may?"

She smiled and agreed, and thanked him sincerely for an enjoyable day, then drove away, free of distractions, thinking once more about Juan and the way he had so cynically tried to detach her from his uncle.

For the next few days she worked as hard as possible. Juan went out most evenings and spent his days in his boat, so they rarely met. Gene tactfully forebore to comment, although he could not have avoided noticing the coolness between them when they did happen to meet, the careful politeness when speech was necessary, and hasty departure of one or the other as soon as it was practicable to do so.

She was learning more about Gene, and her sympathy increased. After Mary died he spent five years working and playing hard, building up his reputation as an actor and also as a playboy. No woman had been able to hold his attention for more than a few weeks, though many had tried. Then he met Louise. She was a year older than Gene, had been married twice, and had sons by both her husbands. Within a month, of meeting her, to the amazement of his friends, he married her.

A year later Louise bore a daughter and Gene's life was transformed. He was seen no more in night clubs and the favourite play spots of rich Californians, but spent his free time with his child. He might have been regarded as a model husband and father, yet as Pippa typed the reminiscences she found that Gene was constantly blaming himself for failure in the early years.

"I spent too much time and attention on Lulu, and made Louise jealous. She accused me of treating her just as a child-bearing machine, and refused to have another child. Perhaps she was right. One of her attractions when we first met had been her triumphant motherhood."

Such passages as these on the tapes, and the bundles of letters Gene produced that he and Louise had exchanged, made painful reading. Pippa wondered whether he would gloss over this very personal aspect of his life and concentrate on his career. There were plenty of incidents here too, rows over casting, the petty jealousies of rival stars, and one or two inexplicable sudden endings of films Gene was working on, work abandoned, the actors and technicians paid off or transferred to other work without explanation.

It had been a bad time for Gene, and Pippa thought it was an effort for him to remember them, although he persisted and threw himself into work as energetically as she.

While he rested in the afternoons Pippa took to driving to explore the island, but it was uninteresting by herself. David took her out occasionally, and although he made his admiration plain he ventured no more than a farewell kiss when he parted from Pippa. She was grateful to him, for pleasant though his company was his kisses stirred her not at all. He might have shaken hands with her for all the response she made. There was none of the delicious shiver of excitement and anticipation that Juan's very nearness aroused. Once or twice she wondered whether Juan had spoiled her for any other man, then crossly told herself that she needed time to forget that love.

The first week, however, made her feel

the loss more intensely rather than less. On Saturday Gene said that he must take a break and he insisted that Pippa did too. She was spending Sunday with David, and since he had to meet a colleague who was coming out to join him she had no plans for the day.

"Maria, may I take some food? I feel like walking and staying out the whole day," she asked, wandering into Maria's spotless, excellently equipped kitchen after breakfast.

Maria swiftly packed some rolls and paté, tomatoes and oranges, and a small flask with chilled white wine.

"Stay out all day, tire yourself out with walking, you have looked pale the last few days," she advised. "You have not been sleeping well?"

"No," Pippa admitted.

"The nights are hot," Maria nodded, but Pippa was aware that it was not the temperature of the air which kept her restless but the fever in her body for Juan's kisses.

She set off aimlessly along one of the ill defined paths leading across the heathland, pausing to admire the many flowers, purple and yellow and blue, which gave colour to the grey-green bushes. Occasionally she glimpsed gaps in the cliffs on her left, and once or twice was tempted to venture to the edge to see whether she could find a way down to the beach. Eventually she found a path leading downwards into a pleasant looking bay, but when she was half way down a motor launch chugged into the bay and disgorged a dozen noisy youngsters who carried air beds and rugs and picnic hampers, and were clearly all set for a long stay.

Hoping that she had not been observed, her jeans and blue shirt merging into the background, Pippa retreated and walked further along the top of the cliffs. She sat looking out over the calm sea to eat her picnic, and then slowly began to retrace her steps.

She had almost reached the Casa Blanca, but was not ready to go back, when she discovered a steep narrow path leading to a beach little bigger than a small room, enclosed by high cliffs which almost totally obscured the narrow opening to the sea. Facing westwards, the sun was still on it, and Pippa stripped off her jeans and top. She was wearing her black bikini underneath and she swam slowly about the small cove for a while, then flung herself down on the sand and let the sun dry her body.

Suddenly her misery overwhelmed her. The isolated cove, the sun, sea and sand, reminded her unbearably of the day she had spent in a similar cove with Juan, and sobs shook her.

After the first wild agony her sobs quietened and brought a certain release from tension. With her head resting on her arms, face downwards, she eventually fell asleep, a brief dreamless oblivion for a short half hour.

Then her cramped arms awoke her and she rolled over, momentarily puzzled to remember where she was. She lay rubbing her arms to restore the feeling, and groaned aloud as memory returned.

"Shall I help?" a soft voice asked, and Pippa sat up in alarm.

"Juan!" she exclaimed. "How did you get here?"

He was sitting a few feet away from her, cross legged on the sand, wearing only a brief pair of swimming trunks. At her question he grinned.

"I swam here. I often do, it's only a short distance from our bay. I take it you walked," he added, nodding to her small heap of clothes beside her.

"Yes," she said, embarrassed now to be alone with him, the first time since their quarrel.

"I'll walk back with you, but first, my sweet, I must talk to you. No, please listen," he said as Pippa, with a gesture of refusal, got hurriedly to her feet.

"What is there to say?" she asked dismally. "I'd rather go back by myself."

She stooped to pick up her clothes, but as she straightened up Juan caught her hands in his.

"No, don't fight me, little one. I could force you to stay and listen but I don't want to have to. If you still want to go back by yourself afterwards then I won't force my company on you, but you must give me the opportunity to explain."

"What is there to explain?" Pippa asked coldly, but she ceased struggling, realising the uselessness of it, for his lean

163

hands were like bands of steel about her wrists.

"Sit down again," he ordered, and meekly she obeyed. He dropped to the ground a yard away and sat looking out towards the sea.

"Well?" she demanded after the silence grew uncomfortable.

"Pippa, I understand about your need to show that you can do a job without the support of your family. I asked you to give up the one with Gene for his sake. I have been thinking over what you said and admit that I was wrong. It would cause him more worry to employ someone else, which is what he would have to do. But it would be a disaster if his book were ever published."

"Why?" Pippa asked, her heart beating erratically as he talked, and it seemed that they were no longer at loggerheads with one another. "Lots of people write down their memories, and people love reading them."

"Gene's life has been somewhat turbulent, and there has always been a great deal of gossip surrounding him. It has died down the past few years, since he retired and has been living quietly here, but to publish his book would stir up everything. If it were done while he still lived he would find the publicity, and the hounding of reporters, very distressing."

"Surely he realises the risk of that?"

"He is stubborn. How far have you got with the typing? Are you doing it in order?"

"More or less," Pippa answered slowly. "Sometimes the tapes are out of order because Gene didn't date them all, but he listens to the first few minutes and gives me the ones about his early life to type first, putting the others aside for later. We've missed a few but he says it can all be sorted into order later, and then he can begin editing and deciding what should go in."

"How far have you got?" Juan repeated.

"About five years after he married Louise," she replied.

"Then you haven't reached the worst part," Juan said slowly. "You know that Louise died, and their daughter?"

"Yes, I'd heard that, but Gene has not mentioned it yet. I don't know when or how."

"That is less important than the rumours and accusations made at the time. Lulu died when she was ten, she was thrown from the new horse Gene had bought for himself. He was out but her nurse, who usually looked after her when he was not there, maintained that she had been sent off for the day. Louise said that he had been with a woman, with all the implications of that. He said he had not sent the nurse away and was interviewing the woman for a small part in a film he was directing. But then Louise claimed that he had always been unfaithful to her, and that Lulu was not his child but the daughter of a lover she had had at the time of her marriage to Gene.

"I didn't believe the story, neither did the people who knew Gene well, but that sort of mud sticks and it would be stirred again if he were once more in the limelight."

"How horrible," Pippa whispered.

"But that is not all," Juan went on sombrely. "Louise died a short while afterwards in a car smash, and her brother claimed that she had told him Gene was trying to kill her and had

166

already tampered with the brakes of the car a month earlier. He missed being officially accused by a hairsbreadth."

"Poor Gene. I don't believe a word of it!"

"No, but you can see that people who don't know him will revel in all the murky details. Even if he dies before it is published it will hurt many people who were badly hurt at the time. Gene has a certain simplicity, he thinks that if he tells his side of the story again, as he did at the time, people in general will be more ready to listen than they were then. I think otherwise."

"But he won't stop writing his book. It is not always a painful experience for him," Pippa asserted.

"No, but I have come to believe that instead of leaving him to find a new assistant it would be better for you to stay on and try to influence him against including certain things. Then if the book is ever finished it might be less damaging."

"I couldn't work against him," Pippa protested.

"I'm not asking you to sabotage the

book," Juan replied, rolling over and taking her hand in his, causing her to tremble with renewed agitation. "I want to help Gene and you can do so too. When you see what he has written I am sure you will see ways of omitting the worst passages, persuading him that his account of the film business in the forties and fifties will be more valuable than personal gossip, dredging up old malice of others against him."

"I might," Pippa conceded.

"That's all I ask for now. And that you stop treating me like a villain. I hate seeing you so unhappy, my dear, and most of all I hate not being able to take you in my arms and hold you close to me and kiss you, like this."

Gently he pulled her to him and slowly, with infinite care, brought his lips down on hers. Pippa closed her eyes and sighed, and her arms stole round his neck as she clung to him, all else forgotten in the bliss of once more having him close to her.

His hard body, still wet from the sea, pressed against hers as he tightened his arms about her, and she shivered in ecstasy as his flesh touched hers. They lay there side by side on the sand and Pippa returned Juan's kisses, willing the moment to last for ever.

It was not until much later, in bed that night, that she realised that in all his murmured endearments, on the beach and after dinner when they had strolled in the garden long after Gene had gone to bed, he had not once uttered the word 'love'. He had not said he loved her or called her his love, or made any plans further ahead than the following day.

Vaguely disturbed by this she tried to shrug it aside and enjoy the moment. It must be enough for her, this short idyll. He would never suggest marriage to her. He had reached the age of two and thirty without marrying, and there must have been many other women who had in the past hoped as she did now. It must be enough for her to enjoy his company, his kisses and caresses, for so long as he chose. The heartache would come later but she did not see how she could avoid it. To cling or demand promises would drive him away.

So it was with a determined resolve

to live for the moment that she went with him early the next morning to his powerful speedboat.

"We'll soon be in Puerto Soller," he said as he cast off. "It's too far to go to Palma today, and back. We need at least a couple of days to see the main sights there. Puerto Soller is a very lovely spot, though, and we will have lunch in the Hostal Es Port, an old fortified manor. It was built to defend the inland town against Arab raiders."

Pippa stood in the bows, her head thrown back as she revelled in the breeze through her hair and the spray on her face. To her right the Minorcan coast slid past rapidly, and they soon passed the Cape d'Artruch.

"We now head straight for Cape Formentor. The drive along that peninsula is spectacular, the land is mountainous along the north coast and then drops for hundreds of feet into the sea."

Momentarily Pippa thought of Sally-Jayne in her hotel, then thrust the thought away from her.

"So Majorca is mountainous. How else does it differ from Minorca?"

"The produce. Oranges, olives, almonds. None are cultivated on Minorca apart from a very few in gardens. There are vast groves of all of them and in February the whole island seems to be covered in pink blossom. People visit especially to see it. I have a liking for the olive groves though. Some of the trees are ancient and incredibly gnarled, with that misty greeny grey colour of the bark which casts a gloom even on the brightest days. One can understand legends and mysteries and ghost stories being invented by people who live permanently beside such places."

"It sounds fascinating."

"You must see more of it before you go home. You should spend at least a week here, there is so much to see."

Pippa was silent, reflecting that his assumption that she would soon return home confirmed her view that he meant no more than a holiday flirtation with her. Despite her efforts she could not turn her mind away from thoughts of their eventual parting.

"See the high cliffs?" Juan asked, for they were now running along the northern coast of Majorca, and Pippa gazed in awe at the vast rocky structures.

"It's forbidding," she said with a shudder.

"Nature is more impressive than even prehistoric man," Juan said, laughing. "Taulas and pyramids can be explained, although we marvel at the skills used by our ancestors. It must have been some gigantic upheaval that thrust these cliffs out of the sea."

Pippa, however, was not listening. She was recalling with horror that she had promised to meet David that morning, and in the bliss of her reconciliation with Juan she had completely forgotten that he existed.

8

"**C**AN I make a phone call?" Pippa asked as they stepped ashore.

"It's almost lunchtime, you can phone from the Es Port."

They walked up the hill to the hotel, its tower dominating the port area. Climbing up through the gardens, past the swimming pool, Pippa acknowledged what a superb position it was in for defending the whole valley which stretched back towards the high ridge of mountains cutting off this northern section from the main part of the island.

They passed through a wide archway, Juan explaining that a small chapel still existed on one side, into an open patio, the centre of the house. While Juan talked to the owner who was clearly an old friend, Pippa was led to a telephone.

She telephoned David's hotel but he could not be found. In the end she left a message saying that she would contact him the next day to explain her failure to meet him. And that, she thought ruefully, would be a difficult task. No man would appreciate being told that he had been forgotten simply because a more desirable one had distracted her attention. She sighed. At least she would have until tomorrow to devise some tactful way of making her apologies without inventing lies.

Juan had ordered sherry for her and they sat in the old room where the olive press still had pride of place, then ate in the terraced restaurant open to the air and the superb view across the bay and to the hills around. Afterwards they walked for a while along the beach and quays and Juan insisted on buying her an embroidered, lace edged blouse and a string of beads made from the lovely grained wood of the olive trees.

"It is a flourishing industry here, carving bowls and salad servers and other small wooden items from olive wood," he said when she admired the vast displays in the souvenir shops.

"I like the leather goods, too. I have

a fancy to buy a leather pants suit like one I saw in Mahon. It was a gorgeous red and beautifully soft."

"Go to one of the fashion shows. They hold them regularly in the tourist season. When we get home I'll give you a card to take to a firm I know."

Soon he said that they ought to be setting off again if they were not to be late for dinner and regretfully Pippa agreed, wondering whether she would ever again see this enchanting island, so different from its neighbour.

David accepted Pippa's stumbling apologies and when he asked her to dine with him the following night she felt obliged to accept. The days flew past, working hard on the tapes each morning, swimming or boating with Juan in the afternoon, and dining out with him a couple of evenings as well as once with David.

Gene's tapes had reached the account of the death of his daughter and it was much as Juan had said, although Gene blamed himself unreservedly for having trusted the nurse who had, whether by mistake or carelessness, permitted the

175

venturesome child to attempt to ride the half broken horse.

She felt that she was breaking no confidences when she tried to explain this to Juan when they were dining in a small intimate restaurant in Cuidadela.

"He could not blame himself more than anyone else."

"I know, although I was too young at the time to know much about it. It is an old, painful wound, and I don't wish him to reopen it. Do you think he is still determined to publish?"

"Yes, but there is so much material that he will have to cut out a great deal. He might be persuaded to leave out most of this personal history."

"Let us hope so. Pippa, if Gene can spare you on Friday shall we go to Palma for the weekend? We could leave on Thursday afternoon, tomorrow, and have two and a half days there, and get back in time for you to work again on Monday morning. What about it?"

Pippa glanced at him warily and he laughed suddenly.

"Separate rooms, in different hotels, if you wish," he said with a light mocking note in his voice. "It isn't that I don't want to take you to bed, child," he added, and she blushed furiously, "but you must not feel any obligation to me! That would ruin any pleasure we might have in each other."

When she did not reply he swiftly changed the subject, but as she lay in bed that night she had to admit to herself that she would offer very little resistance if Juan did suggest their sharing a bed. He had enthralled her so much that she no longer cared for anything apart from the touch of his lips, feather light or hard and demanding, according to his mood, and the feel of his arms about her and his hard chest crushing hers.

She was alone the next morning, for Gene had gone to Cuidadela and Juan was out in his boat, when there was a gap on the tape she was working on. Gene must have left it on again, she thought, and began to flip through it to see whether he had recorded anything else. Then Gene's voice came again and she prepared to type once more. But the words held her still, her hands poised above the keyboard.

"Come in, Juan. It's almost time for dinner, I've booked a table at the Savoy."

The Savoy, Pippa thought. In London? Could this have been recorded during that visit when she had first encountered Juan?

"Did you engage her?" Juan's voice came, curt and sounding angry.

"I did, my boy. A pleasant, nice little thing. She'll be a joy to have around the house."

"That is obviously what she hopes."

"What do you mean?" Gene asked, puzzled.

"When I left here earlier I had the doubtful pleasure of overhearing part of her conversation with some rejected suitor. She was being perfectly blunt with him, telling him of her plans to marry a senile old man for his money. Since the only elderly man in view must be yourself, you clearly figure in her mercenary plans!"

Pippa gaped in astonishment. She recalled her angry words to Frank outside Gene's London hotel suite and also the fact that almost immediately afterwards she had found Juan in the doorway behind her. He could have overheard those words but how dare he interpret them as he had done.

"Nonsense," Gene was saying on the tape. "You are imagining things. Just because Sally-Jayne was a gold-digging little slut doesn't mean every girl is. I'm going. Coming?"

There was no more. The rest of the tape was blank but Pippa sat staring at it for a long time, clenching her hands together as she strove to control her furious anger.

Suddenly she sprang to her feet and disregarding the papers that fluttered to the floor she ran out of the room and through the house. From the terrace she could see that Juan was in his boat moored to the jetty, and she ran as fast as she could across the beach towards him.

Seeing her in such haste he sprang down and ran to meet her.

"What is it? Is someone hurt?" he demanded.

She stopped a few yards away from him, her breasts heaving.

"No. You — you are despicable!"

she declared. "How dare you say such things of me? Why, you didn't even know me then, you'd only seen me for a moment. How could you accuse me of such — such underhand, such p-perfectly horrid designs on Gene?"

"Pippa, sweet, what is all this?" Juan asked, half laughing and stepping towards her, his hands outstretched.

She leapt away from him.

"Don't you dare ever lay hands on me again! Oh, you must have thought it a great joke to make love to me, thinking that you could distract me from my plans! I suppose you hoped I would think you a better catch, like Liz says Sally-Jayne does! No, keep away from me! I hate you and your nasty suspicious mind, and I never want to see you again!"

Juan came purposefully towards her and although, seeing the implacable determination in his face, she turned to flee, suddenly afraid, he caught her by the shoulders.

"Calm down," he said softly, but with a certain menace in his tone, and shook her slightly. "What crazy notion have you got into your head now?"

Pippa gulped and wriggled but he held her firmly, his fingers biting into her shoulders.

"I — I heard the tape," she whispered. "One of those Gene uses. He left it on — he often does — and it was in London."

"Well?" he persisted.

"You accused me of trying to — to marry him! You said you had heard me saying I wished to marry a senile old man, you said that I wanted his money! You said I was mercenary!"

"I seem to have said a great deal," Juan commented. He spoke lightly but Pippa sensed the anger behind the casually uttered words and began to wish that she had never come out here to him. The water was frighteningly near and he was strong. She thought his grip on her could never be loosened, so rigidly was he holding her, and now his eyes blazed down into hers and she could not read their expression. She shivered and tried to look back at the house to see if anyone else was watching, but it was deserted. Only Maria was there in any case. Anger came to her rescue.

"You did indeed!" she flung at him. "It must have amused you seeing how easy it was to entice me away from Gene. If you think I am devious what about yourself? Gene is worth two of you! He says what he means and I'd rather — rather — oh, I hate you!"

His hands had suddenly relaxed their grip and she wrenched herself away from him. Afraid that her tears of anger and frustration and disappointment would overflow at any moment, she seized the opportunity to run and to her relief he did not attempt to follow her. She locked herself in her room, pleaded a headache when Maria came to tell her that lunch was ready, and gratefully accepted a tray in her room that evening.

When she emerged the following morning, pale and with dark rings round her eyes, it was to find that Juan had gone.

"He's always unpredictable like this," Gene commented. "He didn't say where he was going or when he'd be back, but I know he has to go to America in a couple of weeks so I hope he will be back soon."

Pippa did not. She could not bear to see him again for he had not denied his suspicions of her, or his efforts to distract her from her supposed plans regarding his uncle. While her body craved his touch, her mind insisted that it would be better for everyone if they never again met.

"Does he plan to stay in the States for long?" she managed to ask in as near normal a voice as possible.

"I believe so, several weeks, then he will probably go to London."

Angry, confused, and missing him bitterly, Pippa somehow lived through the next few days. When David telephoned to suggest that she spent Saturday with him she listlessly agreed, and together they explored more of Mahon and the Villa Carlos. When he kissed her that night she did not repulse him, although she found no comfort in his tender embraces.

"Tomorrow?" he asked, releasing her. "I have to see someone in the morning but I could call for you after lunch."

"Yes, do that, David."

"I ought to be thinking of moving on in a couple of weeks," he said. "How long is this job of yours likely to last?"

"I have no idea, there is still a great deal to do."

"I shall be on Majorca for a while. Perhaps you could come across for a few days before I go back to England?"

She nodded. It really did not matter. Although David was pleasant undemanding company she took little pleasure in sight seeing with him. With Juan it had been so different.

She spent Sunday morning finishing some typing and then she and Gene sat on the terrace together having a pre-lunch drink. As Gene was telling her his plans for the following week, when he hoped to have the bulk of the typing finished and could start editing the material, they heard a car approaching.

Pippa looked up eagerly, forgetting for a moment their quarrel as she looked for the familiar Mercedes, but it was a hired car.

"Some friends who've put into one of the harbours, I expect," Gene said, but he started up from his chair in surprise as the visitor walked out onto the terrace.

It was Sally-Jayne. Dressed in white, as

she had been on her last visit to the Casa Blanca, her deep tan and voluptuous figure, together with her lovely face, ensured that in any company she would be noticed.

"What a surprise," Gene said coldly. "I thought you did not wish to see me again?"

"What a delightfully polite welcome!" Sally-Jayne flung back at him. "I came to see whether you had come to your senses at last."

"I am not giving way to your demands," Gene said curtly.

Sally-Jayne sat down, crossing one long leg gracefully over the other. She completey ignored Pippa.

"You still intend to publish those lies about me?" she asked in a silky voice that held more menace than her previous angry tone.

"I shall publish the truth," Gene replied. "Now, since there is nothing for us to say to one another, I suggest you leave."

"Not until I have tried to change your mind."

Gene sat down again in his chair. "You

cannot," He said wearily.

"I want a drink. Luis, get me a Martini."

Pippa looked round, surprised. Luis, who must have answered the door to Sally-Jayne, still hovered nervously in the drawing room window. He looked dubiously at Gene.

"Get her something, Luis," Gene ordered, and Luis disappeared.

"Good. I expect it is too much to expect you to ask me to lunch," Sally-Jayne said sarcastically. "Never mind, what I have to say will only take a few minutes."

She took the drink Luis brought to her with a nod of thanks, drank half of it in one swallow and turned back to Gene.

"You said when I came here before that it didn't matter to you what I said about us. Very well, there is an alternative. But in case you believe that I do not intend to tell my version of the story, I'll tell you that I've spent the last few weeks writing it down. I've brought a few pages with me, just to give you the flavour!"

She dragged a foolscap envelope out of

her large handbag and flung it towards Gene. He made no attempt to catch it and it balanced for a moment on the edge of the table, then dropped to the ground.

"There are other copies of all of it with my London and my Los Angeles solicitors, and they have instructions to release them to the press as soon as your book's publication date is announced. It is not just about us although there's plenty I can say about that! I've been talking to Louise's elder son."

Gene's eyes narrowed but he did not speak. Sally-Jayne drank the rest of her Martini and put the glass down on the table.

"At the time it was only her brother who was suspicious, and he had no proof," she went on slowly, enunciating each word clearly. "It was bad enough when Louise revealed that instead of looking after Lulu you'd been frolicking with a teenager in a garden chalet so that Lulu got on that wild horse and was killed, trampled to death after she'd been thrown. If you'd been there Gene, either it would not have happened or you might have had a chance of saving her. Has that thought kept you awake at nights? Was it that which gave you nightmares during our marriage? Was that why you shouted out Lulu's name in your sleep?"

"Stop it!" Pippa burst out, unable to bear the look of pain on Gene's face. "Do you have to be so vindictive?"

Sally-Jayne turned to her and looked her up and down superciliously.

"Is this your latest conquest, Gene? You always did like them out of the cradle. But she's not so young or so pretty as the one you were with when Lulu died. Why do you like your mistresses to be so young?"

"Please leave," Pippa asked curtly. "If you have nothing to say except abuse then it is better that you go or there will be another scandal!"

"Are you threatening me? My, you are sure of yourself! But I doubt if Gene will marry you, pet, you're not really his type, not sophisticated enough, too little glamour. And he wants that as well as youth and innocence."

"Pippa is worth a dozen of you," Gene said slowly, and Pippa noticed that he

188

was gripping the arms of his chair so hard that his knuckles were white.

"I haven't finished. As well as Lulu there is what happened to Louise. I know you bamboozled them into disbelieving what her brother said because there was no proof. Her car was burnt out, no-one could tell whether it had been tampered with and no-one saw the crash, or knew whether any other vehicle had been involved. They had to let you go for lack of evidence, despite what Louise had told her brother earlier. A great pity he repaired her brakes himself then, for he could produce no evidence of that. But I can."

She lifted her glass to her lips, realised that it was empty and set it down again angrily. She glanced triumphantly at Pippa.

"Louise kept a diary. You didn't know that, did you Gene? But it went to her elder son with other personal things and he has sold it to me. I can prove by her own words that you tried to kill her! I have her diary!"

"Get out of here, you lying little whore, before I tell Luis to throw you out!"

189

Gene said furiously, rising to his feet and taking a step towards his former wife. "You won't intimidate me with your threats and lies, I still intend to publish the truth and no vicious little devil like you is going to stop me! Now go."

He turned away and stumbled slightly, and Pippa sprang across to help him. Behind them Sally-Jayne laughed.

"How touching! Youth and crabbed age. It isn't worth it, child, not for all his money. Far better to make certain of a young man, a virile one. And there are some rich ones about, too, if you could snaffle one. I have one last piece of news, Gene dear, then I'll go. Juan and I are to be married in a few days."

Gene had stood silently until then, supporting himself between Pippa and the table. At Sally-Jayne's final words he swung round quickly and tried to speak. As he opened his mouth he raised his hand as if to strike her, but no sound came from him except a strangled groan, and he suddenly crashed to the ground in front of her with Pippa helpless to prevent his heavy weight from falling.

"Luis! Maria! Come quickly!" Pippa screamed as she dropped to her knees and felt for Gene's pulse. It was sluggish but he was still alive. She struggled to lift his head, from a gash on which blood oozed, and suddenly Luis was beside her.

"Maria, the doctor, telephone at once," Luis snapped out, and felt for Gene's heart. "Can you take his legs, Miss Dawson? It is a very short way to his room and he would be better in bed."

Pippa was strong although small and she and Luis managed to carry Gene across the terrace and through the french windows into his bedroom. There she left Luis to do what he could and marched back onto the terrace. Sally-Jayne was still sitting where she had been all the time, but she eyed Pippa warily as the latter walked purposefully up to her.

"You have caused enough trouble. If he dies I'll see to it that you pay for your part in it, Sally-Jayne Ross! Now go and don't come back here, ever!"

"The lioness with her young?" Sally-Jayne quipped, but her voice wavered slightly and she rose slowly to her feet.

"There is no point in staying now, is there? But do continue to persuade him, if he recovers, that to publish would be a very foolish thing to do. You need not see me out, I used to live here."

She strolled through the drawing room and Pippa followed purposefully. She stood by the front door watching the hired car as it disappeared through the gates, and then turned to find a white-faced Maria leaning against the kitchen door.

"The doctor? Is he coming?"

"Yes, miss, he was at a house not far away, and his wife will telephone him there. Miss, lunch is — "

"Lunch? Oh, no, Maria. I must go and see if I can do anything to help Luis."

She found Gene lying on the bed, deathly pale and still unconscious, but Luis said that he was breathing more steadily. They sat watching him, powerless to help, not speaking. Then the sound of another car was heard and Luis went to bring in the doctor.

After a rapid examination the doctor was reassuring. Luis translated quickly for Pippa's benefit. The attack had been a warning but was not going to be fatal. With careful nursing and provided that he remained in bed for some time, and was not worried, Gene would recover. Indeed, under the doctor's ministrations he recovered consciousness and was able to understand what had happened to him.

After a while the doctor left and while Pippa remained beside Gene, Luis took him out. Pippa heard some conversation in the hall but it was a babble of Spanish and she could not understand it, so ignored it. Luis seemed to be a long while returning and Gene had dropped into a quiet sleep when he did come back.

"Miss Dawson, please come outside for a moment," he whispered with an anxious look at the bed.

"What is it?" Pippa demanded as soon as they were in the hall.

"Maria, she was running to the telephone and she fell over. She has broken her arm. The doctor has set it but she says that she cannot serve your lunch and will not be able to cook dinner. What are we to do?"

"Maria? Oh, poor woman! She looked so white but I thought it was just shock. I'll come to her at once. Is she in bed?"

"She would not, she is worried about the vegetables, she says they are overcooked because she forgot to turn them off until just now. She says they are not fit to eat."

"Nonsense! Where is she?"

Pippa finally reassured Maria that she would not starve and could even eat overcooked vegetables if necessary, then persuaded her to retire to bed.

"I can cook for now, I used to enjoy cooking, and we can get a maid soon, surely? Just until you are better again. Luis, do we need a nurse for Mr Watson? Did the doctor say anything about that?"

"He is sending one. There is an agency we can try in the morning for a maid. I can look after Mr Watson until the nurse comes. Thank you, Miss Dawson. Ought we not to tell Il Conde?"

Recalling Sally-Jayne's announcement of their marriage which had so enraged Gene, Pippa swallowed hard.

"Do you know where he is?" she asked,

and Luis dolefully shook his head.
"He did not say."
"Do you know where he could be staying on Majorca? He might be there and we could telephone likely hotels or friends if you know their addresses?"
Again Luis shook his head.
"There are so many."
"Well, try a few, someone might be able to tell us. But first we must all eat."
"Yes, miss, I'll lay the table at once."
"No, I'll eat here in the kitchen. Take a tray to Maria and then come and eat yourself, then you can try telephoning. Heavens, who is that?" she exclaimed as the doorbell rang.
Luis went to see and came back to announce that a Mr Nightingale had called for her. Pippa exclaimed in dismay.
"David! Come in here," she said, finding him standing in the hall looking rather puzzled. "Luis, an extra glass. David, do sit down and I'll explain. I'm sorry, but I can't come with you, there's been an accident. Two, in fact."
She explained and David provided

enormous help and comfort. He insisted on helping her prepare dinner for the evening and did not appear the slightest bit put out to have his plans disrupted yet again. They managed an hour on the beach before Pippa was called back to the house, and after she had seen Gene briefly they cooked dinner together.

"Will he recover?" David asked as they sat with coffee afterwards on the terrace. "He's got a weak heart anyway, I believe?"

"Yes, but the doctor seemed to think it was not too serious an attack. He is worried, though, about his book. I've promised him I will continue it without him until he is allowed to start work on it again, and that made him easier. But with Maria's broken arm as well and no certainty that we can get a maid at once, or that she'll be useful when she comes, I shall be busy."

"And unable to come out with me," David finished ruefully.

"I'm sorry, David, I really am, but there's nothing else I can do."

"Of course not. May I come out here after dinner each evening, just to see you? Then if there is a chance for you to get out for a while we could walk or drive."

"Come to dinner, not afterwards," Pippa suggested impulsively, knowing that David's company would help her to relax and hoping that it would help to take her thoughts away from Juan, and the bitter hurtful news that he was to marry Sally-Jayne.

David eagerly agreed and then, saying that she looked tired, took his departure.

Pippa was emotionally exhausted but she knew that she would not sleep, so she sent Luis to bed saying that she would curl up in the large, comfortable armchair in Gene's room and keep watch over him.

"You cannot sit up all night," Luis protested.

"It won't hurt me, I can doze."

"I will take a turn with you after I have slept for an hour or two. Call me if you need any help."

He went, and Pippa had finally to face her thoughts. Only the still figure of the man in the bed prevented her from giving way to her despair at the shattering of every last hope. Juan's suspicions might have been explained away, indeed he might have done so at once if she had not let her fury rule her, but now he was committed, and she would never again feel his arms about her, his hands caressing her, or hear his voice whispering tender nothings. This quarrel could not be made up.

9

PIPPA was too busy the following day to brood about Juan's marriage with Sally-Jayne. Luis had come to her at two o'clock and insisted that she went to bed for a few hours, but she had slept badly and risen early to see to breakfast for everyone. Maria was running a slight fever and Pippa insisted that she remain in bed to recover from the shock.

Gene was pale and weak, and when Pippa carried in his tray of coffee and toast he caught feebly at her hand.

"Don't let them persuade you — to give up," he managed to whisper. "I'm not giving — in!"

"Of course not, but you are not strong enough to work again yet," she said gently as she helped him to sip the coffee.

"You can — go on — for a while?" he asked slowly.

"Yes, of course, I can finish the typing

and possibly begin to arrange everything in chronological order," Pippa reassured him. "If you promise to stop worrying and concentrate on getting well again!"

He smiled and seemed content, and fell into a light daze as she was tidying his room. She met Luis in the kitchen who reported that he had not been able to trace Juan anywhere on Majorca.

"Never mind, he may come back any time. When will the nurse be coming?"

"The doctor said that he would bring one when he came to visit Mr Watson this morning."

"Good. I'd better prepare a room. What about a maid?"

"I will telephone the agency as soon as they open. Then I had better fetch some stores. I will ask Maria what we need."

"I think she is sleeping. Let's go through the stores in the kitchen and make a list."

Luis went off to telephone while Pippa explored the cupboards in the kitchen, finding her way around and checking the stocks of the various foods. When Luis came back to report that there was a maid available on the following day she already had a list for him.

"Are any of these in some place I haven't seen?" she asked, and he went swiftly through the list with her.

"No, Maria keeps all of these in the kitchen. There is a big cupboard next to the laundry, full of tins, and the freezer, so we won't need these," he said, striking through a couple of items. "Is there anything I can get for you?"

"No, thank you."

"Then I will go now."

He left in the small Seat car and Pippa went upstairs to find a suitable bedroom for the nurse. The first two she tried were connecting rooms joined by a bathroom, so she passed on. Then she opened the next door and found that Juan occupied a similar suite of rooms, although he had made the second bedroom into an office with a table near the window.

Feeling uncomfortable, as if she had been prying into his personal affairs, Pippa hastily left the room and found a small single bedroom next door which was perfectly suited to the nurse. She checked that the bed was made and towels ready in the small bathroom off, and blessed Maria for her competent housekeeping. The house was always ready for guests, it appeared, so there was nothing much for her to do.

She looked in on Gene but he was still sleeping, as was Maria, and after jotting down menus for the next few days she went into the study and began to type.

A few minutes later the doctor arrived and Pippa let him and a tall thin elderly woman in. The nurse spoke a little English and the doctor knew a few words, so they were able to communicate after a fashion and Pippa was relieved to find that the doctor was satisfied with Gene's progress.

"In bed, always, no worries, no noise, understand?" the doctor said to Pippa, and gave copious and rapid instructions to the nurse, who nodded briefly and immediately began to establish herself in the sickroom.

"Coffee for both of you?" Pippa suggested, and the doctor smiled and nodded. The nurse accepted with a brief nod and made it plain that she would stay with her patient. Pippa took the doctor to the drawing room and had just carried in the tray when Luis arrived.

With a sigh of relief the doctor broke into voluble Spanish, obviously giving Luis many instructions, for he kept nodding in comprehension, and then the doctor took his coffee, drank it quickly, and after thanking Pippa briefly, departed.

The nurse was brusque but clearly competent, and Pippa was thankful that one worry was lifted from her shoulders. By the time David arrived and insisted on rolling up his shirt sleeves and starting to prepare the vegetables she was content that all would be well.

The nurse refused to join them for dinner, preferring a tray in her room, and Pippa could not help being glad. She was so curt and her English was so limited that it would have been an uncomfortable meal. Luis said that he preferred to join Maria, who was now feeling much better and was anxious to get up, so Pippa and David ate alone in the breakfast room.

"Luis would not permit me to eat in the kitchen again," she said with a laugh, "but I persuaded him that it would be more sensible to use this room instead of the dining room, which is so formal and rather too grand for just two of us."

David grinned, and chatted about his work so that Pippa could relax and forget her problems. She almost fell asleep as they drank coffee on the terrace, and David made her promise to go straight to bed when he stood up to leave.

"May I come again tomorrow?" he asked, and she nodded eagerly.

"Please do, it's such a relief to have someone else to talk to."

He departed and Pippa went wearily upstairs, and slept deeply. In the morning she felt physically refreshed, although the emotional turmoil of the past few days had not diminished. She hoped that she would be kept too busy to think of Juan.

The maid arrived midway through the morning. She was only seventeen, came from a small village in Andalucia, and had hoped to get employment in one of the large Majorcan hotels. They, however, needed no new staff until the main summer influx of visitors, and Ana had been working for the owner of a villa who had just returned to Germany. She was small, dark, willing but untrained, and after a couple of hours Pippa was beginning to think that it would have been less trouble to have done everything herself.

All her instructions had to be translated by Luis, and then Ana usually misunderstood them, and did not seem to be able to follow Pippa's demonstrated examples so that it had to wait until Luis was around again before further explanations could be given. And Ana could not even cook. She had happily said that she would make salad and cook tortilla for lunch, but Pippa had sat down to lettuce which had not been shaken so that it was limp and watery, with a dressing consisting mostly of oil and nothing else, and tortilla burnt underneath and uncooked on top.

Unwilling to starve at dinner also, Pippa set Ana to washing bedlinen and clothes, supervising the operation of the washing and drying machines, and leaving Ana happily folding clothes and sheets and arranging them in piles, while she began preparations for dinner.

Again she went exhausted to bed, but

happy in the knowledge that Gene was rapidly regaining his strength. When she went downstairs in the morning she found Maria, wrapped in a voluminous cotton dressing gown, sitting in the kitchen and issuing abrupt orders to Ana.

"Maria! How are you? Should you be out of bed?"

"I'm well enough, Miss Dawson, and I can do some things one-handed, and Ana here can do the rest. Don't worry, Miss Dawson, she understands me all right!"

Pippa grinned suddenly. Ana did seem much happier under the autocratic style Maria had adopted, and Pippa reflected that she had probably grown up in a large family where her mother would have issued orders rather in the same manner as Maria was doing. She went to see Gene and found him sitting up in bed while the nurse shaved him.

He smiled at her and then grimaced comically as the nurse ordered him to keep still. When she had finished and removed the towels and bowls he patted the bed.

"Come and sit down, my dear. I'm sorry to have given you this fright but

Luis tells me you are coping admirably. Are you finding enough typing to keep you busy?"

"Yes, there is plenty to do," Pippa said, thinking that she had in fact had little enough chance to carry on with that work. Now that Maria had recovered and was able to supervise Ana she should be able to catch up with it.

She left soon afterwards and went into the study, remaining at her desk until mid afternoon, when she went into the kitchen to see if there was anything she could do for dinner. She found Ana chopping onions and peppers while Maria, one-handed, operated the mixer while she watched Ana carefully.

"Maria, you should be sitting down," Pippa told her sternly but Maria laughed.

"This is no effort and Ana does anything which needs two hands. We can't have Il Conde going without his spice cake, can we?"

"Il Conde? Is Juan back? Where is he, I had not heard him."

"He and that woman arrived a few minutes ago, they are upstairs unpacking."

Pippa's eyes widened. She had no doubt who 'that woman' was.

"She is staying here?" she demanded. "Does Mr Watson know?"

"He does not," Maria replied grimly, "and I told Il Conde that I did not care whether she came with him or not, I would not have her upsetting him again. He has promised that she will keep out of the way and they will only be staying a few nights. Something about being on the way to Madrid and then America. Good riddance to her, I say."

"Did he know his uncle was ill?"

"Yes, she told him, he said."

"Well, he's taken long enough getting here," Pippa snapped, and turned to leave the kitchen. Suddenly she could not bear to talk to anyone. Sally-Jayne had said that she and Juan were to be married in a few days. Surely he would not have brought her here until his uncle was better if he had realised that it was the argument with his ex-wife which had brought on Gene's attack? Perhaps they were already married, or on their way to be married in Madrid.

She almost ran out of the house and

down to the beach. Her eyes were so misted with tears that she did not realise until she was almost at the jetty that Sally-Jayne and Juan were standing on it, looking down into the speedboat tied alongside.

It was too late to turn back and so she blinked away her tears hurriedly and stood looking at them.

"Well, well, the faithful companion," Sally-Jayne sneered when she noticed Pippa's presence.

"I came to ask you not to permit Gene to know you are here," Pippa said in a tight little voice, addressing the other girl. "He is very ill and it would worry him."

"You take a great deal on yourself issuing orders here!" Sally-Jayne said angrily. "I shall do as I wish and if I want to see Gene you are certainly not going to stop me!"

"The orders are from the doctor, for Gene to be kept absolutely quiet with no noise and no worries," Pippa replied, hanging on to her temper by a mere thread.

"Oh, the little watchdog now. Will you

bite if I come too near? Do you want to preserve what you think you have won?"

"You are talking nonsense," Pippa snapped. "I am concerned that Gene has the opportunity to get well, and I hope that you will also make that your first concern," she added curtly, turning to look at Juan for the first time.

Her heart nearly burst. He was wearing a pale grey suit in the finest worsted material, a white shirt and a silvery grey tie. Just the sort of suit a man might wear to go on his honeymoon, Pippa thought dully. Sally-Jayne wore a pale grey dress edged with white lace, and white accessories. It was almost as though they had deliberately dressed to match. She thought wearily of the old jeans and plain tee-shirt she wore herself, and the contrast between her own simple attire and Sally-Jayne's elegance was almost more than she could bear. She scarcely listened to Juan's reply as he said sharply that he thought he could be trusted to know what was best for his uncle.

"Darling, can't you see, she's afraid," Sally-Jayne purred, slipping an arm possessively through his. "Afraid that her neat little plot to make herself indispensible to Gene and then marry him when he is too ill to resist her will be spoilt. She must have had a fright when he collapsed, thinking that it was too late and she had missed her chance to get all his money."

Pippa suddenly saw red.

"You jealous bitch!" she shouted at Sally-Jayne. "How dare you say such things when you did your best to kill Gene? You can't bend him to do what you want any more, and you are determined that he shall have no more happiness! You are selfish and spoilt and wicked! I mean to see that Gene's last few months are happy despite you!"

Turning suddenly she left them and ran for the house. Panting as she reached it, she looked round hurriedly for Luis, and was thankful to see him bending over the Seat, fiddling with something near one of the wheels.

"Luis, please, come and help me to tell the nurse something," she gasped, and taking his hand almost dragged him into the house.

"Wait here, we must not disturb Gene," she told the surprised Luis, and went quietly along the hall to Gene's room.

He was asleep and the nurse was sitting quietly beside him reading. Pippa beckoned to her and she got up and left the room.

"Luis, explain, please, that Sally-Jayne is here, that she caused Mr Watson's attack and must on no account be permitted into his room, and he must not know that she is here!"

Swiftly Luis translated and then smiled reassuringly at Pippa.

"Do not worry, the nurse and I will make sure he is not disturbed. I will tell Il Conde that it might be fatal for him to see her."

"I think it might," Pippa said worriedly.

"Don't worry," he repeated. "It is almost time to lay the table for dinner. Is your friend Mr Nightingale coming tonight?"

"Dinner? I will not sit at the same table!" Pippa said vehemently.

"Il Conde told me that he is taking — the other one — out to dinner," Luis said soothingly and Pippa breathed a sigh of relief.

"Thank goodness. Yes, Mr Nightingale is coming. I'll go and change."

In a mood of defiance she dressed in the long gold and brown dress she had worn for her first date with Juan, and took special care with her hair and face, putting on more makeup than she normally used and drenching herself with her most expensive perfume. She was half way down the stairs when a sound from above caused her to look up.

Juan, in evening dress, and Sally-Jayne in a figure-hugging white silk dress with deeply plunging neckline, were coming along the upper hall. Pippa turned and hurried down the stairs, feeling unable to face them. She went along the lower hall to stand outside Gene's room, and watched as the couple went out of the front door without a backward glance. As she heard the Mercedes being driven away she heaved a sigh of relief, and softly went in to make certain that Gene was comfortable.

"Hello, my dear. Are you going out

with Juan? You look very pretty," Gene said.

"I — er — thank you, Gene," Pippa said in confusion. So Juan had seen his uncle, but it was clear that no-one had mentioned Sally-Jayne's presence. "How are you feeling now?"

"Better, thank you, but sleepy. All the nurse does is feed me with sleeping pills," he chuckled.

"You need your rest. I'll leave you to sleep now. Good night, Gene."

She crept out of the room and went to the kitchen. Dinner was almost ready and Maria nodded to her reassuringly.

"How do you feel, Maria?"

"Tired, Miss Dawson, but otherwise all right. I shall go to bed when dinner is over. Ana can manage the washing up."

At that moment the bell rang and Pippa went out into the hall to admit David. He was carrying a large box of chocolates and a bunch of roses.

"I bought you these," he said with an unusual bashfulness, handing both box and flowers to her.

"David, how kind!" Pippa exclaimed, and smiled brilliantly at him. After the past few days, and the blazing row with Sally-Jayne earlier, together with the nagging desire to know whether she and Juan were yet married, it was comforting to be cosseted like this. Luis brought a bowl and she arranged the roses while David drank a whisky. Then Luis announced dinner and they went through into the small breakfast room.

Somewhat to Pippa's surprise it was an excellent meal, and she thought wryly that Maria had more skill in managing Ana than she had shown herself. It would make her own life easier, though, and she could keep faith with Gene by carrying on his book.

They lingered over coffee and then strolled into the garden, for it was a hot night and airless indoors. David was so sympathetic a companion that Pippa suddenly found herself pouring out all her anger and fears about Sally-Jayne's effect on Gene. Concealing her own love for Juan, which she knew had not changed whatever he had done, and her fears that he was by now married to Sally-Jayne, she told David how the other woman had threatened to publish damaging and probably untrue accusations about Gene if he persisted in writing his memoirs.

"Can you be sure all his recollections are truthful?" David asked.

"No more than anyone's own view of matters," Pippa said slowly, "but she was so vindictive, and would have gloated if he had fallen dead at her feet! Gene has been the victim of so much malice and so many rumours. They have prevented him from reaching the top in his profession and he wants to tell his side of it all. It is all he has left, David."

"It's not your decision in any case, my darling. Come, let's walk down to the water and then I must go."

Later, as they returned to the house, David slipped his arm round Pippa's waist.

"I shall be leaving Minorca a week tomorrow," he told her. "I shall miss you more than I'd have thought possible a few weeks ago."

"Leaving?" Pippa exclaimed in dismay. Without realising it she had come to rely on David's undemanding friendship and the thought of losing it now, just when she needed all the support she could find, was a great blow.

"I'll be in Majorca for a month or so. I hope you will come and see me there, or I could come here for weekends if you feel you can't leave Mr Watson. And I'm hoping that you'll come to England for a while before you finally go home."

"I don't know. I can't promise," Pippa said slowly. "I shall miss you too, David, and I'd like to see you again. Perhaps we could arrange something before you go next week? I should know more then, whether I could leave Gene for a day or so." And I will have suffered the final parting from Juan, she added to herself.

"Sweet Pippa," David murmured and took her into his arms. She went unresistingly, and turned up her face for his kiss. He kissed her for a long moment and then, with a whispered promise to be with her the next evening, he turned away to his car.

Pippa watched him drive away and then turned to go through the front door. She had her hand to her lips and her eyes half closed, recalling the very different emotions she had felt when Juan had kissed her, and she jumped in alarm when Juan's voice came out of the darkness.

"Have you twisted another poor sucker about your little finger now?" he asked harshly.

"What — what do you mean?" Pippa demanded, astonished.

"Don't play the innocent with me! It won't serve you any longer, I've at last come to realise what you are!"

"Be quiet! You'll wake Gene!" Pippa hissed at him.

"Gene! A fat lot you care for him despite all your protestations!"

Pippa tried to push past him but he caught at her arm and held her in a cruelly tight grip.

"Let me go, you're hurting me!"

"Not until I've said what I have to say."

"Then say it in here where Gene won't be disturbed," Pippa replied furiously, and turned towards the drawing room.

Somewhat to her surprise Juan came with her willingly enough, and released her as soon as they were inside. He snapped on the light and stood leaning against the door, surveying her sardonically as she blinked in the brightness, absently rubbing her arms where his hands had gripped her so violently.

"What is it?" she demanded coldly.

"You are a little tramp!" Juan said slowly. "First that boy in London, then me, now this fellow, and all the time you are making Gene think you the little innocent. Well it won't work. You'll not marry him!"

"I'm not — " Pippa began furiously, but he did not allow her to finish.

"You go out with that poor fool while Gene is helpless. I know it is not in your contract to care for Gene, nor do you have any duty towards him while he is only your employer, but you might consider his feelings just a little. He cares for you, deluded as he is, and you have the nerve to claim that you will make him happy! By heavens, you are a deceitful little whore!"

"I care a great deal more for Gene than you appear to, bringing your wretched woman here with you!" Pippa flung back at him.

Juan took a menacing step forwards and Pippa backed nervously away, puzzled and afraid of the look in his face.

"Gene may get well enough to marry you, he may even recover his powers sufficiently to bed you!" Juan said through gritted teeth, "but I'll make damned sure you'll regret it! How can a woman like you be satisfied with an old man? Does the money make up for it? How much do you want to leave him alone? Tell me what your price is and I'll pay it to you."

Enraged, Pippa suddenly struck out and caught him by surprise a glancing blow on the cheek.

"If Gene wants me, I'll marry him!" she declared hardly aware of the sense of her words, but so inflamed by Juan's accusations that she did not care what she said so long as she could hurt him as much as he was hurting her.

"You'll regret it if you do," Juan said, but so quietly that Pippa scarcely heard him.

He took another step towards her and she found herself backed against the arm of one of the chairs. When he grasped her by the shoulders she tried to wriggle free but could not evade his grip.

"I'll show you what a real man is like," he muttered, and Pippa felt a glow of sheer terror overwhelm her.

As Juan bent towards her she tried to break away from him, but he bent her over the chair and in order not to lose her footing she clutched at his arm.

Suddenly she found herself pulled into a close embrace and felt his breath on her cheek. Then as she opened her mouth to cry out in fear his lips came down on hers.

She struggled but he held her powerless, and she could not even kick him because her legs were pressed hard against the side of the chair. His mouth was hard and she felt bruised, unable to breathe, and her senses were swimming. Then she felt him relax and slowly, sensuously, his lips softened and moved gently against hers, then his mouth was against her throat while his hands, no longer holding her imprisoned, gripped her waist and his thumbs traced the line of her ribs.

For hours, it seemed to Pippa, they stood there embraced. She no longer

221

wanted to scream or to escape him. Although she knew that he was furiously angry with her, and she fully returned that anger, she had thought never to feel his lips on hers again, and the bitter sweet ecstasy of it reduced her to a quivering bundle of senses, without any will or volition of her own.

She stiffened momentarily when he drew down the zipper of her dress, but he let his lips travel over her neck as he slid the gown from her shoulders, and she shivered as she clung even closer to him. The dress fell to the floor and she suddenly found herself swung up into his arms. He carried her swiftly across the room and laid her down on one of the huge, soft settees beside the fireplace. Then he knelt beside her and began, agonisingly slowly, to kiss her throat and neck, gradually moving nearer the swell of her breasts.

Completely forgetful of what had led up to this Pippa was conscious only of the desire flooding through her body, and she moaned as his lips agonisingly tantalised her.

"Juan, Juan, I love you! Juan, don't leave me."

Suddenly fearful that he would move away she clung urgently to him, her arms about his neck, and sighed in satisfaction as he moved to lie beside her on the settee, twisting to enable their bodies to meet.

As he kissed her again and again he held her close to him, one hand hard against her back while with the other he traced the line of her jaw and neck and shoulder. Her breasts were crushed against his chest and she was gazing into his eyes, pleading with him to satisfy the craving he had aroused in her when he suddenly gave a sigh and sat up, calmly pushing away her hands as they clung to him.

"Juan," she protested weakly, and then the realisation of what had almost happened flooded over her, and aghast at her own abandoned behaviour she turned her face into the back of the settee and tried to muffle her sobs in the cushions.

"Pippa," Juan began, but she shook off his hand from her shoulder, uttering a cry of loathing.

"Go away!" she cried, but her voice was smothered by the cushions, and she knew only that his hand was no longer there.

Some time later she looked up to discover that she was alone and Juan had switched off all except one small table lamp. Ashamed, she struggled into her dress again and made her way cautiously through the dark, sleeping house until she reached at last the security of her room, and crept miserably into bed to lie wakeful, castigating herself for her unprecedented behaviour and trying to suppress the wayward regret that Juan had left her when he had.

10

WHEN Pippa went downstairs the next day she found to her relief that Juan had gone out in his boat and Sally-Jayne was having breakfast in her room. She drank several cups of strong coffee but could not eat anything. Then she went to see Gene.

He was sitting up in bed looking much stronger and with more colour in his face. He looked at her with concern and abruptly turned to the nurse and dismissed her.

"Pippa, my dear, what is wrong between you and Juan?" he asked bluntly.

Pippa looked at him, startled.

"Why — why, what should be wrong?" she parried. She was puzzled. Had he forgotten what Sally-Jayne had told him, that she and Juan were to marry? He must have done so to speak as he did. Perhaps it was for the best, but she would need to be cautious so that he was

225

not reminded of it.

"I claim the privilege of an old man, my dear, to interfere," Gene went on firmly. "It has been perfectly clear to me that Juan finds you attractive and I cannot blame him. I think you are a little in love with him too, and so it disturbed me when I heard you quarrelling last night. My door was open a little, I heard you in the hall and then some time later Juan went out and you went to bed, but your steps were so slow, so dejected, I thought, that it concerned me. Won't you confide in me?"

"I — yes, I have enjoyed his company. Juan is a very pleasant companion, he is handsome and attractive," Pippa said in a strangled voice. "But it is nothing. I — he feels no more for me than — than a girl to flirt with! And he is going to America soon. It is all over, not that there was anything more than — friendship."

"I will respect your confidence, my dear. Do you want to go back to America too? You could see him there, you know."

"Oh, no, I couldn't follow him!" Pippa exclaimed in dismay. "Please, Gene, I would prefer not to talk about it."

"Very well, if you will answer me one more question, truthfully, with no evasions. Have you quarrelled because of my memoirs?"

"He — does not like them, he — thinks they will hurt you," Pippa said slowly.

"You have not answered me. Has Juan asked you to stop helping me?"

"It would make no difference to him if I did, and I will not give up!" Pippa exclaimed.

"I see," Gene murmured as if to himself. "Very well," he went on in a more normal voice. "We will talk of it no more. But I would like you to go into Mahon for me this morning to buy presents for Maria and Luis. It is their wedding anniversary next week and I thought I would like to give them something early to make up for Maria's accident and all the extra trouble I have caused them. Maria has a passion for luxury bathsalts; get her a huge jar and also powder and body lotion, and perfume. You will know what to get. And Luis has been secretly longing for a velvet jacket. Look, I have written down his measurements on this piece of paper. Get green or red, the brightest you can. Here is a cheque that you can cash at my bank. If you need more spend it and I will pay you back afterwards."

Pippa nodded, took the paper and cheque Gene had ready and left the room. She ran upstairs to change from her jeans into a light pleated white skirt and yellow shirt, and then went out to the garages. As she drove the Seat through the gates she saw Juan walking slowly up from the beach, and congratulated herself that she had not met him.

She blushed painfully when she thought of the way in which, last night, he had so aroused her senses that not only had she forgotten her anger with him but had shamelessly indicated that he might do to her exactly as he pleased. Her abject submission to his skilled lovemaking must have sickened him in the end, too, she thought miserably, for she could think of no other reason why he had left her so abruptly after reducing her to nothing more than a mindless shell, at his mercy and totally responsive to his desires.

She hoped that she would be able to avoid both him and Sally-Jayne until they left, which might with luck be within the next day or so. She could not look him in the face again, and yet never again to see him was desolation.

Angrily she thrust his image away from her and concentrated on planning what to buy for Maria. The cheque Gene had given her was a very generous one, and unless the jacket cost far more than she expected she would have plenty of money for all manner of bathroom luxuries for Maria.

She parked the car in Mahon's Plaza de la Explanada, cashed the cheque at the bank nearby and then walked towards the maze of narrow streets in the old quarter of the town where there was a good choice of shops.

Luckily she found a rich dark red jacket for Luis almost at once, and so was able to spend time selecting the most suitable range of gels and talcs and other scented luxuries for Maria before the shops shut for the long lunch and siesta. She had not realised how late it was and came out with her last purchases just as the shops were all closing.

There was no need to rush back so Pippa found a small cafe where she could sit outside under a vine-shaded pergola and eat lunch. Then she took her parcels and walked slowly back to the car. She was reluctant to return to the Casa Blanca for fear of meeting Juan, but there was no alternative and she set out.

The house was quiet when she arrived, and after taking the parcels up to her room to give to Gene later, Pippa went to find a cool drink from the fridge. She took it out onto the terrace and sat under one of the sunshades, sipping slowly, then she went into the study to carry on with the typing.

The first odd thing she noticed was the absence of the portable tape recorder which Gene used. After searching the study in case someone had placed it in a different position she shrugged. Possibly Gene had persuaded the nurse to fetch it for him. He used it sometimes to play music tapes and she might, dragon as she was, have permitted that.

It did not matter, Pippa thought, for

there were still several notebooks which she had not started. She opened the drawer where they were kept and found that it was empty. Hastily she looked in all the drawers of the desk, and found that while the ordinary items had been left undisturbed the notebooks and tapes, all of them, both those she had typed and the others, had vanished. So had the various bundles of letters Gene had been working on.

Pippa sat back slowly. It had never seemed necessary to lock the desk, there wasn't even a key as far as she knew, but it seemed plain that someone had stolen all the tapes and books. Was it Sally-Jayne or Juan? Had they, failing to persuade Gene to give up his plans, taken this despicable way of defeating him?

Shaking with anger she started up and was half way to the door when she recalled that the typing she had done was stored on the disks of the word processor, and she swung back to switch it on with trembling fingers and call up the last few pages she had done. But the screen remained blank, and when she looked in the disk drive she found that new disks had been inserted and all the ones she had already used had, along with the tapes, vanished.

Pippa whirled out of the door and ran up the stairs to Juan's room. She knocked peremptorily and after a brief pause flung open the door. The room was empty and she could see through the open door of the bathroom that he was not there either. A hasty look out of the window showed her that his balcony was empty, but a sunhat and pair of sunglasses lying on the table seemed to indicate that Sally-Jayne was occupying the other room in the same suite, which shared the balcony.

She no longer cared, Pippa tried to tell herself, and then she caught a flash of white down on the beach, and saw that Juan was by the boats. Turning, she left the room and hurried out and down to the beach.

Juan looked up at her, unsmiling, as she slowed to a walk a few yards away from him. He did not speak, merely lifted his eyebrows in what Pippa thought was a supercilious manner. Damn him! She would not remember last night or bother wondering what he was thinking.

"Where are the tapes?" she demanded.

"What tapes?" he asked curtly.

"Gene's. All of them and all his notebooks, and the disks and every copy of what has been done have been stolen! Have you taken them, or that — or Sally-Jayne?"

"I can't think why you should imagine that I am a thief," he replied frostily, and in her imagination Pippa could see hordes of his proud Spanish aristocratic ancestors standing beside him, so haughty was his manner. If she had not been so furiously angry she would have shrivelled to a cinder under his gaze, she thought afterwards. But at the time she did not care and stared back at him wrathfully.

"You've given me no cause to think well of you!" she snapped. "You are arrogant and despicable and I hate you."

"As you did last night?" he asked softly, and Pippa's face flamed.

"You should be ashamed to even think of it!" she raged. "How could you have behaved so, with your w — " she gasped, but it hurt too much to say, and so she substituted, " — with Sally-Jayne waiting

233

for you upstairs? Where are the tapes?"

"I have no idea. By the way, your fiancé arrived this morning."

"My fiancé — who do you mean?" she demanded in astonishment.

"Frank, I believe his name is. He told Gene that he had come to take you home, that you were going to marry him. Gene is rather disappointed that you should choose a young man after all, but he understands. It will be best for all of us if you go as soon as possible, and make up your mind which man you want!"

Pippa turned away dazed. Frank here! Part of her anger turned towards him. How dare he come and tell Gene that they were to be married? She began to run back towards the house and in the hall she met Nurse Teresa.

"Mr Watson, is he awake?" she asked breathlessly.

"No, he sleeps. Later you see him."

Pippa had to restrain her impatience for another couple of hours until Maria came to tell her that Gene wanted to see her. She hurried down to his room. He looked tired but he smiled at her as she

234

approached the bed.

"I did all the shopping," she said in as normal a tone as she could.

"Thank you, my dear. You have been a great comfort to me."

"I — I am not leaving you!" Pippa exclaimed.

Gene shook his head.

"I thought that it was Juan you loved. This young man, your fiancé, you have never talked of him."

"He is not my fiancé and never was!" Pippa said vehemently. "His father and mine are partners and it has always been assumed that Frank and I would marry one day. But I left London because I would not agree, I wished to be on my own for a while. He has no right to claim otherwise!"

Gene looked at her closely and then smiled slightly.

"I confess he did not strike me as the right one for you, but then I would prefer to support Juan's claims!"

"Please! I have said Juan does not love me. Where is Frank? How dare he follow me!"

"He is staying in an hotel in Cuidadela,

and he said he would come to see you tomorrow. I thought that if you wished to go home you could make arrangements then, but if it is true that you do not intend to marry him I hope you will stay here for some time."

"I — of course I will, there is — " Pippa stopped, recalling the odd disappearance of the tapes. "Your book!" she exclaimed in dismay.

Gene sighed.

"You have worked so hard on it, my dear, but it is all over now."

"You know?" Pippa asked, relieved that she did not have to break the news to him. "What happened?"

"I destroyed them. I have decided that Juan is right, publication of my story would create an unnecessary suffering for so many people and what, after all, does it matter to me?"

"How? When?"

"This morning. Nurse Teresa was my accomplice. I am afraid I sent you out of the way deliberately, my dear, this morning, for fear my resolution should fail me. But I would like you to stay for a while all the same."

"I — I can't!" Pippa exclaimed. "Did Juan know what you'd done?"

"I told him when I saw him after lunch."

Pippa's head was spinning. Why, if he knew the truth, had Juan not told her when she had accused him? Then the answer hit her with the force of a blow. He did not care what she thought. He was so proud, so certain, that her suspicions and her opinion mattered nothing to him.

"Please, I must think!" she whispered, and Gene nodded understandingly.

"The doctor agreed that I could have visitors now. I saw that young man this morning but I would like you to have dinner here with me tonight. Juan can fend for himself for once."

Pippa bit back the reply that he would be fully occupied with Sally-Jayne. Gene did not know that she was in the house. She nodded and escaped to her room.

What could she do? She would certainly not return to California with Frank, and she did not even wish to see him after his action in claiming her as his fiancée. Equally she could not remain here. The

237

purpose for which she had come no longer existed, and despite Gene's pleas she could not bear to stay where everything would remind her of Juan.

Suddenly she had a longing to tell Dolores everything, and in London she could try to forget before she faced her family and Frank again. How soon could she get away?

She went down to the study and telephoned to the airport. After some delay she was told that there was a flight late the following afternoon direct to London, and a spare seat.

"We cannot hold it for you after tonight," the voice warned, and Pippa suddenly made up her mind.

"I'll take it," she decided, and put down the receiver slowly. This was the end.

As she dressed in the misty blue dress that evening, she resolved not to tell Gene that she intended to leave. It would hurt him, of that she was sure, but she would leave a letter to explain her reasons as far as possible. She could not bear to cause an argument on her last evening and she knew that he would be sure to try to dissuade her.

There remained the problem of how she could get to the airport. She could order a taxi but that would not allow her to depart unseen. She decided reluctantly that she would have to take Luis into her confidence, at least partially, and so she went in search of him.

She found him washing the large car outside the garages.

"Luis, is anyone using the Seat tomorrow morning early?" she asked.

"No, Miss Dawson. Do you want it?"

"Yes please. I shall be leaving soon, now that Mr Watson has decided not to complete his book, and so I wanted to see as much as I could of the island. I've never been to Monte Toro," she added slowly. "I can't leave without seeing that, everyone tells me how superb a view one gets from it."

Luis looked at her curiously and nodded.

"I will leave the car for you."

"I mean to go very early before it gets too hot, and before Mr Watson wakes. He would say that I must go later but I — prefer to go early."

"I will not mention it to him if that is what you prefer, Miss Dawson," Luis assured her, and Pippa escaped before she had to begin inventing explanations for her strange conduct. Luis probably assumed that she wished to be back in order to do some work for Gene, but that could not be avoided. She would have to ring from Mahon airport to tell Luis where the car was, and beg his forgiveness for the trouble it would be collecting it, but it seemed to her the only way.

She went slowly back to the house and saw Sally-Jayne going through the front door. Pippa delayed, not wanting to encounter the other girl, but when she reached the hall Sally-Jayne was nowhere in sight and Pippa was able to go straight to Gene's room.

He seemed determined to forget all causes of dispute and kept the conversation on impersonal topics. Pippa did her best to respond but she was thankful when the nurse came in and said that it was time for Mr Watson to go to sleep.

"Good night, Gene, sleep well."

She dared make no other farewell, but she sat up for hours composing a letter which she would leave in the car for Gene, telling him how greatly she had enjoyed working for him and how sorry she was to have left in such a fashion.

"I am sure that you will understand and forgive me," she finished.

Then she packed her cases, but even after the long exhausting day she could not sleep. Over and over in her mind she passed from one incident to another of her dealings with Juan, from the first angry meetings to the delightful and tender interludes before she had realised how he was trying to detach her from his uncle. But always her thoughts reverted to the previous evening, his expert kisses and the wild desire that had surged through her veins. Never could she feel that desire for any other man, she thought dolefully. She had loved Juan, did still love him, she admitted to herself. Whatever he had done did not alter that. Nor did the thought that he had never had any feelings of love for her.

At last she slept fitfully, tears streaking

her face. In the morning, long before the rest of the household awoke, she crept down the stairs and let herself out of the door. Piling her cases into the car she started it quickly and drove as fast as she could away from the Casa Blanca, her last view of the bay being through the driving mirror.

She reached the turning to Cala Santa Galdana and suddenly thought of David Nightingale. He had been coming to the Casa Blanca the previous evening but had never arrived. She wondered why not. There had been no message, and in the stress of the day's events she had completely forgotten that he had said he would come.

Glancing at her watch she realised that it was still long before breakfast time. If she drove to his hotel she would be able to speak to him and say goodbye before he had to go out for the day.

She arrived at the hotel and the receptionist telephoned David's room. Within a few minutes he had joined her in the cool, marble floored hotel lobby, and they sat on the side of the ornamental fountains in the centre.

"I came to say goodbye," she said baldly. "Why didn't you come last night?"

"I received a message that you could not meet me," he said, puzzled. "You did not send it?"

She shook her head.

"So much happened, or I would have telephoned to see whether you were all right. Who could have sent the message?"

"Never mind, you are here now. Come out to dinner tonight. I have to attend an important site meeting today but I should be free by six."

By six o'clock she would be on her way to London, Pippa thought sadly.

"I'm sorry, David, but I'm going — home," she substituted at the last minute. She did not wish David to find her in London if she was still there when he returned. It was unfair, she could offer him nothing and it was unkind to let him hope.

"Home? But why? Has the old man — is he worse?"

"No, he is much better but he has decided not to do the book after all, and so there is no point in my staying.

I want to leave as soon as possible."

"I understand, it must be frustrating to have the work stop like that," David sympathised.

He could not know the other frustrations she had suffered, Pippa thought wryly. But David spoke again.

"I'm sorry we can't see some of Majorca together. Are you sure you won't stay on?"

Pippa shook her head.

"You are kind but I must go," she replied firmly. "I have so much enjoyed your company, David. Thank you for all the comfort you have been to me."

"You'll write? Please, Pippa?"

"Yes, I'll write," she agreed, thinking that it would not hurt to do that at some time in the future.

"Will you have breakfast now? Have you time?"

She shook her head hastily. She had all the time in the world but she could not sit down in a crowded hotel dining room and make polite meaningless conversation.

"I must go," she said, a note of desperation in her voice, and mercifully David did not argue. He walked out to the car park in front of the hotel with her and she drove away, across the little river that gave the name to the cove, up the sweeping road, and on her way once more.

Almost immediately she forgot David, but he had reminded her that she had several hours to fill before she need go to the airport. Then the excuse she had given Luis occurred to her. Why not, she thought. She had never visited the Monte Toro and a church, especially one which had been used as a sanctuary over the years, might give her some of the peace she craved.

In Mercadal she followed the signs leading through the town and up to the church. At the last moment she stopped and bought some rolls and fruit, for although the thought of food nauseated her she must try to eat something.

She drove slowly up the serpentine road, narrow and steep, and edged with walls to hold up the higher stretches and prevent them from sliding onto the lower reaches, but with little on the edges to save unwary drivers from hurtling down to the bottom of the hill.

When she reached the top she was glad that she had bought some food, for it was too early to visit the sanctuary. She wandered to the edge of the car park and sat on the wall overlooking the road she had just come up, and ate the rolls. Then she walked to the highest point outside the church and looked at the surrounding country, the pattern of stone walls clearly outlined to the south.

Leaving the tall statue, arms outflung as if to embrace the whole island, behind her she eventually walked through the gateway, past the statue of the group around the cross, and the well, and in through the lovely archway and the tiled entrance where huge pots of green plants were beautifully placed.

For a long time Pippa remained in the cool, soothing interior of the small chapel, and then when the first group of tourists appeared she went in their wake up the steps to the terrace high above the chapel, and stood looking towards the capes and bays to the north, oblivious of the clicking cameras and loud voices of the people around her.

There was no more to see and it

was still very early. How could she fill in the many hours before her flight left? Shopping? She had no present for Dolores, and she could buy small souvenirs for her parents. Postcards, too, to remind her of the days when she had once dreamed of happiness.

The other tourists were filing through the gate at the top of the stairs and the plump little nun was looking across at her expectantly. Pippa began to cross towards her but the nun was looking after the last of the tourists who had just passed her, and then she stepped back to let someone through before moving away from the gate and leaving Pippa alone with the newcomer.

11

PIPPA stared disbelievingly. She must be dreaming. How had Juan known she was here? At the furious look in his eyes she stepped back but there was no escape for her.

"What do you want?" she managed to say in a hoarse voice.

"Why are you leaving Gene?" he demanded, coming to a halt a foot in front of her as she pressed back against the parapet.

"What business is it of yours?" she demanded, suddenly strengthened by her anger.

"I want Gene to be happy."

"And you think forcing him to give up his book will make him happy?" she asked scornfully. "You have gotten your way over that, so please stop interfering and leave me alone!"

"I did not know that he intended to destroy all the tapes," Juan said mildly. "I did not wish him to publish, true,

248

and I am glad that he has come to see it my way, but I happen to believe it is for his good. But that is beside the point. Why were you leaving in such a secretive manner?"

"I have no job now!"

"Gene has not dismissed you."

"There is no work to do."

"Yes, there is. You know that Gene has only a few months to live. This attack could have made it less. I intend to see that his last weeks are made as happy as possible. If that means that you stay at the Casa Blanca, then you stay."

"Oh, you arrogant fool! Do you think you can coerce me into staying? You are off to America soon, you cannot imprison me against my will."

"I, to America? No, I will remain if necessary. But I do not think it will be."

"You can't keep Sally-Jayne hidden for months in the same house," Pippa protested.

"She will not be there. But I shall. Come, don't be foolish. I withdraw my opposition. I see that Gene needs you. You are not to be permitted to run away from him."

"I was not running away!" she said with a groan, and knew that it was untrue.

"Then why take all your clothes? The cases are in the Seat, and I intend to drive you back. Don't think you can escape me. Luis has already cancelled your seat on the plane."

"Luis? Did he give me away? But he didn't know I was leaving!"

"It was not difficult to deduce when we found your room empty. We phoned the airport and found that you were not leaving until this afternoon, and then Luis mentioned that you had said you wished to visit Monte Toro. We drove here. Not very difficult after all, I think you will agree."

"Please, go away!" Pippa said, turning away from him and staring unseeingly across the island.

"I beg that you will not force me to carry you down to the car. I am quite prepared to do so if you will not come willingly," he warned, and Pippa knew full well that he was perfectly capable of carrying out such a threat.

"And this was once a sanctuary," she

said bleakly. "But I doubt whether that would have stopped you!"

"My dear girl, what the devil do you mean by objecting? I offer you what you have wanted from the beginning and you refuse it. You have only to keep Gene happy for a short while, and then you will be a rich widow and you can choose another husband as soon as you wish."

She gaped at him.

"Widow? Just what is it that you are suggesting?"

"I've had quite enough of this display of innocence," Juan snapped. "You set out with the idea of marrying Gene, senile though you may mistakenly have thought him. I began to believe that I was wrong but you tried to tell me that you cared for him, that you proposed to make him happy and would pay no heed to my objections."

Pippa was frowning at him, utterly bewildered, and he uttered an exclamation of disgust.

"When I tried to buy you off you refused," he said in bitingly slow accents. "You said that if Gene wanted you then you would marry him!"

Vaguely Pippa recalled saying something like that in her wild anger, and she blushed vividly. Juan turned away from her swiftly.

"I offer you no more resistance. Gene does want you, and you must accept what he wishes."

"Has he told you that?" Pippa asked, aghast.

"He does not need to tell me." He turned back to her and advanced a threatening step. "Let us argue no more. It is fruitless and wastes time. Luis has driven the Mercedes back and will make some excuse until I have you there. Come."

He seized her arm and though Pippa shivered to feel his hard fingers biting into her flesh she began to walk towards the door with him as if in a dream. He held her tightly all the way down the stairs and out through the courtyard. The other tourists had gone, their small bus was just negotiating the sharp first bend out of the car park, and there were only two other cars waiting there besides the Seat. Their occupants were inside the chapel or the small shop, obviously, and there was no help to be had from them.

Juan opened the passenger door and thrust Pippa inside. Then he got into the driving seat and adjusted the mirror, not looking at Pippa.

"Put the safety belt on," he ordered sharply, and when she did not move stretched across her to unhook it from beside her. That brought his face close to hers and for a moment she felt him hesitate, and turned away from the look of hatred in his eyes. For the moment she was helpless but there must be some way out of this tangle.

Did Gene really want to marry her? Had he said so? Much as she liked him and pitied him the very thought of marrying a man three times her age revolted her. Surely he could not demand it?

The car began to move and Pippa looked dolefully out of the window. If Gene really wanted her to stay she could, she supposed, but not as his wife. And only if Juan were not there. That would be her condition if there was really no way of leaving Gene.

They negotiated the first few bends, and Juan had to go dangerously near the edge to pass another car making its way up the steep twisting road. Pippa gasped and clutched the seat as she stared down at the sheer drop below. There was nothing to prevent a car from hurtling to the bottom.

They went round another bend and Pippa almost cried out in alarm. She bit her lip to stop herself from pleading with Juan to go more slowly. Was he deliberately trying to frighten her by taking the bends at this reckless speed? Now he seemed to be trying to overturn the car, for the inside wheels were running in the rut at the side of the paved road.

The next bend approached at frightening speed and Pippa watched the stone wall which edged it leap up before her. She heard a scream and closed her eyes, then felt a sickening jerk as at the last minute Juan wrenched the wheel round and somehow negotiated the bend.

"Juan!" she heard herself crying, and realised that the scream she had heard had been her own.

"Hold tight," he said calmly, and disbelievingly Pippa opened her eyes and looked at him. Was he mad, she thought in panic.

He was sitting tensed over the steering wheel, his eyes narrowed, and as she watched in terror he steered the car to the very edge of the road, on the inside of the hill, and deliberately scraped it jarringly against the wall. She thought for a moment that the impact would overturn the small vehicle, but somehow he kept it upright, although the speed did not lessen.

"Stop, Juan, please stop!" she pleaded. "You'll kill us both!"

He flashed a grin at her.

"I'd like to stop, my dear," he drawled, as he negotiated at speed another hairpin bend, bumping the car against another wall and then ricocheting across the narrow road and running with one side in a rough narrow cart track. "Unfortunately," he went on calmly, "the brakes have failed."

Pippa stared at him in horror, and then she realised that he had changed to the lowest gear and the handbrake was full on. The car continued its headlong progress and by a miraculous display of skill Juan kept it on the road. Unable now to close her eyes, Pippa realised how Juan slowed the car as much as possible by scraping it along what walls or ruts offered. She prayed that they would meet no other cars coming up, but she had an odd feeling, now that she knew the problem, that Juan would succeed.

At one point they almost teetered over the edge but Juan hung on grimly and they regained the road. Several more bends were negotiated and Pippa realised that the speed, although far too great for such a road, was not increasing. Juan was to some extent controlling their precipitate descent.

The last bend came into view and the road became less steep. Juan swung the by now thoroughly battered car round it and on to a level stretch of road. Then he gradually eased over towards the offside ditch and the car was dragged to a halt as he steered it over the rough grass and low bushes, finally twisting round to face the way they had come, one back wheel resting in the ditch.

Pippa, for the first time in her life, quietly fainted.

She came to some while later in a small, completely strange bedroom. For a moment she could recall nothing and then the nightmare drive came back to her and she cried out in horror and tried to rise from the bed where she was lying.

"Keep still," Juan's calm voice ordered, and he pushed her gently back against the pillows. "The doctor is downstairs now and you must stay where you are until he has seen you."

She lay back weakly and a tall thin man came into the room followed by a fat, volubly talking woman. He waved to her to be silent and crossed to stand beside the bed, looking down at Pippa.

"You are a very fortunate lady," he said in English. "Are you hurt? Bones broken? Move your arms, please."

Pippa meekly permitted him to check her limbs, take her pulse, and feel for bruises.

"Shock. No damage. Drink this, and when you have slept you may go home."

He dropped a powder into a small

glass of water and lifted Pippa's head so that she could drink the potion. Within minutes she was asleep, and when she woke again she felt quite restored. She pushed away the light blanket covering her and sat up. Juan rose from his seat near the window and crossed to look down at her.

"I am sorry to have given you such a fright," he said formally.

"It was not your fault," Pippa replied in a low voice. "It was your skill that saved both our lives. I must thank you."

He smiled, but bleakly.

"What would Gene have said if I had contrived to kill you?" he asked lightly, turning away from her.

Pippa gritted her teeth.

"I have never wanted to marry Gene, and I am sure he has no such thoughts about me," she suddenly blazed at Juan. "It is all your suspicious imagination! Not everyone is so devious as you are! I hate you, detest you!" she stormed at him and suddenly, to her horror, found tears streaming down her face. She turned sharply away from him, but he had seen.

"Pippa — " he began, taking a step towards her. "Darling, don't cry!"

The unexpected endearment made her sob still more, and suddenly she felt his arms tight about her, and a very comforting shoulder in just the right place to lean her head. Gradually her sobs lessened and she found a large handkerchief placed in her hand.

She struggled upright, wiping her face. "I'm sorry. I didn't mean to do that."

He ignored her apology and took her chin in his hand, turning her face towards him and looking into her eyes.

"Have I been mistaken all this time?" he asked. "Pippa, did you not wish to marry Gene?"

"The idea would never have crossed my mind if you hadn't been so determined on it," she said wearily.

"But, when I first saw you with Frank you said you were going to marry a senile old man."

"A figure of speech. I didn't mean it, but I was angry that he kept following me. I lost my temper. When that happens I say things I don't mean," she confessed.

"I began to believe that," he said

slowly. "As I got to know you I couldn't believe you to be mercenary or heartless. I thought you were beginning to care for me."

She tried to turn away but he held her tightly.

"Wasn't that what you intended?" she asked in a tight voice. "To show Gene how unsuitable, how worthless I was?"

"It crossed my mind, but I soon forgot that. I wanted you to care for me, Pippa, and I believe you were beginning to."

"Wasn't it all to take me away from Gene? Not only from him, but from his book?"

"Only in the very beginning. I still wanted him to stop doing it, but I was so uncertain about you."

"How do you mean?" She dared not look at him.

"I was contemptuous about your motives at first because of what I heard. I also came across a page of a letter, beginning 'My dear Frank,' in the garden."

"It blew off the balcony — I had screwed it up and decided not to write to him," Pippa recalled.

"Not before you had said how excited you were, and that your plans were working out. It made me still more suspicious," Juan explained. "It seemed odd that after your quarrel you were still in touch with him, and discussing plans."

"That was when you began being nice to me," Pippa said slowly. "To show Gene that I was unworthy?"

"I confess it, at first, and I beg your pardon, Pippa. But very soon I found myself attracted to you, against my will. I was confused, uncertain. No woman had ever had that effect on me before, little one," he said softly, his arm tightening about her as they sat together on the bed.

Pippa looked up at him, scarcely able to believe her ears, but he was staring out of the window, a slight frown on his face.

"I went away, partly to think, partly to get away from your influence and try to decide what my feelings really were. I found that I needed you, I couldn't stay away. That was when I came back to take you to the barbecue. I thought it was too late."

"Too late? I don't understand," Pippa exclaimed, trying to disentangle the welter of emotions in her head.

"I walked into the study, and Gene was standing with his hand on your shoulder, and you were looking up at him with a fond expression. It was clear that he was very attached to you, but I could not decide whether you were acting."

"I am fond of Gene, he has been very kind," Pippa said slowly, "but nothing more."

"I was so uncertain of myself, and that is a new experience for me," Juan said with a wry grin.

Pippa laughed. "Yes, I can imagine so," she agreed demurely, and he kissed her lightly on the cheek.

"I knew that I loved you then, but when I asked you to give up your job you were so angry that I did not know what to think about your feelings for me. I was afraid that you were set on marrying Gene, and using me simply for a good time. I was determined then to make you love me."

"If only you had said!" Pippa exclaimed. "I didn't know what you wanted, and I didn't dare imagine that you loved me. You are so handsome, so rich, there are so many girls!"

"Thank you for the handsome bit," he said with a laugh. "But there have been too many girls, and all seemed to be after my money. At least you could not be accused of that while I still thought you wanted Gene. I have more than he does, you see, and will also have his, so I was a much better catch. That is another reason why I thought you might have real feelings for him, and if that were so I could not come between you. He has had too little real love for me to spoil his last opportunity. But then I knew you didn't love him when I saw you with David Nightingale that time. I was mad with jealousy!"

Pippa turned away to hide her blush, but he gently forced her face back to look down into her eyes.

"I am sorry, my sweet, I behaved abominably. I was jealous and thought that if you were cheating Gene you should be made to realise how unsatisfactory it would have been. You had responded to me before and I was vain enough to think I could turn your anger into desire. Then I could not go through with it, I did not want lust without love between us. Darling Pippa, can you ever forgive me?"

"Juan, I wanted you so much," she whispered, and he clasped her to him and kissed her eyes, and then, softly, her lips.

"I was jealous, I sent a message to David not to come."

"So that's why — but what about Sally-Jayne? You came back with her?"

"We met at a friend's house in Majorca and she told me what had happened to Gene."

"Did she tell you that she had said you were going to be married?" Pippa asked indignantly. "I think it was that rather than the threats she made which caused him to collapse."

"Yes, she tried to trap me by telling our friends too. I knew that she had to return to Paris to begin filming, and stupidly I thought she would be safer under my eye here than spreading rumours about us, that is why I kept her with me. It almost killed us both," he said soberly.

"How is that?"

"Haven't you wondered why the brakes failed?" he asked, and as she recalled the nightmare descent from the Monte Toro Pippa shuddered. Juan held her tightly and she took a deep breath.

"Brakes do fail," she said slowly, "but they were all right on the way here."

"I telephoned for Luis to come here as soon as the doctor had seen you. He examined the Seat and found that the brake cable had been partially cut. Gradually the strain would break the rest. Did Sally-Jayne hear you asking Luis to use the car?"

Pippa suddenly recalled following the other girl into the house after she had spoken to Luis.

"She could have done, she was outside. But surely she would not have deliberately tried to kill me?" Pippa exclaimed in horror.

"Sally-Jayne has no compunction. You saw how she has behaved towards Gene. She feared you because she knew how I felt about you. And Luis saw her outside again later, near the garages. The story she heard about the accusations against

265

Gene must have given her the idea. Either that or an incident in a film she was in a year or so back, when she had to do it to prevent the villains from escaping. She would have known how to do it from that."

"There's no proof," Pippa shivered. "Will you ask her?"

"She's left, on her way to Paris. I took her to Mahon early this morning and then I came to find you and your room was empty. Luckily Luis thought of here when we had discovered your flight was not until the afternoon. It was fortunate you had not started to come down."

"I've not thanked you for saving me," Pippa whispered. "No-one else could have driven like that!"

"I'm not going to lose you now," he retorted. "I thought at the time that you had flown because you were afraid of me. I was determined that if Gene wanted you he should have you."

"Gene never did; why, he spoke about you — " she broke off.

He was smiling. "So Gene saw it too? Did everyone know how we felt except the two of us?"

Slowly, lingeringly, he kissed her lips, and then his lips grew harder, more demanding, and Pippa surrendered to the bliss of knowing that her own desire was returned. At last, sighing, Juan released her.

"Here or California?" he asked.

"For what?" she asked hazily.

"Now or next week? Darling, I'm not sure I can wait at all if you look at me like that. No, don't turn away to hide your blushes, they are very charming. I suppose you have doting parents who have always wanted a big wedding for their daughter? They wouldn't consider flying here straight away?"

"Wedding?" Pippa said faintly, still hardly able to assimilate the wonderful fact that Juan loved her, and not yet having spared a thought for whether he would want to marry her or not.

"Yes, my love. Or are you going to find some excuse? I warn you, I won't accept it, whatever it is."

"My head is whirling, I can't think!" she exclaimed.

"Then I'll make the decisions. Gene would not be able to fly to the States for some time, and would not wish us to delay on his account. Besides, the sooner it is done the sooner we can come back here frequently to see him. And I suppose we really must allow your family a part. But they need not have all the bother of arrangements. I'll cable one of my managers to go straight to California and take all the details in hand. Meanwhile we'll have a quiet wedding here in the Casa Blanca, for Gene's sake, fly to Rome for a couple of days to get you a wedding gown, and then they will have had time to have made all the arrangements in California. Where would you like to spend your honeymoon, my sweet?"

Pippa was blinking at the crisp decisiveness he displayed. It was yet another facet of the man she was, so incredibly, to marry. Would she ever know him? Well, there was a lifetime ahead to find out.

"Are you like this when you manage your estates and factories?" she asked with a slight smile.

He grinned appreciatively. "Always, when I know what I want and am determined to get it. Now, my beloved, I know what you want too, and it will be my one desire to give it to you."

She sighed contentedly, leaning her head against his shoulder.

"I love you so much, Juan. I want this moment to go on for ever."

"Unfortunately we cannot deprive the good woman who lent us her bedroom of it for ever, and Luis is waiting to drive us home. And I think, my darling, that you will find some other moments in the future that are even more delightful. I shall do my best to ensure that, I promise," he vowed, looking deep into her eyes.

TO FIGHT THE WILD
Rod Ansell and Rachel Percy

Lost in uncharted Australian bush, Rod Ansell survived by hunting and trapping wild animals, improvising shelter and using all the bushman's skills he knew.

COROMANDEL
Pat Barr

India in the 1830s is a hot, uncomfortable place, where the East India Company still rules. Amelia and her new husband find themselves caught up in the animosities which seethe between the old order and the new.

THE SMALL PARTY
Lillian Beckwith

A frightening journey to safety begins for Ruth and her small party as their island is caught up in the dangers of armed insurrection.

THE WILDERNESS WALK
Sheila Bishop

Stifling unpleasant memories of a misbegotten romance in Cleave with Lord Francis Aubrey, Lavinia goes on holiday there with her sister. The two women are thrust into a romantic intrigue involving none other than Lord Francis.

THE RELUCTANT GUEST
Rosalind Brett

Ann Calvert went to spend a month on a South African farm with Theo Borland and his sister. They both proved to be different from her first idea of them, and there was Storr Peterson — the most disturbing man she had ever met.

ONE ENCHANTED SUMMER
Anne Tedlock Brooks

A tale of mystery and romance and a girl who found both during one enchanted summer.

CLOUD OVER MALVERTON
Nancy Buckingham

Dulcie soon realises that something is seriously wrong at Malverton, and when violence strikes she is horrified to find herself under suspicion of murder.

AFTER THOUGHTS
Max Bygraves

The Cockney entertainer tells stories of his East End childhood, of his RAF days, and his post-war showbusiness successes and friendships with fellow comedians.

MOONLIGHT
AND MARCH ROSES
D. Y. Cameron

Lynn's search to trace a missing girl takes her to Spain, where she meets Clive Hendon. While untangling the situation, she untangles her emotions and decides on her own future.

NURSE ALICE IN LOVE
Theresa Charles

Accepting the post of nurse to little Fernie Sherrod, Alice Everton could not guess at the romance, suspense and danger which lay ahead at the Sherrod's isolated estate.

POIROT INVESTIGATES
Agatha Christie

Two things bind these eleven stories together — the brilliance and uncanny skill of the diminutive Belgian detective, and the stupidity of his Watson-like partner, Captain Hastings.

LET LOOSE THE TIGERS
Josephine Cox

Queenie promised to find the long-lost son of the frail, elderly murderess, Hannah Jason. But her enquiries threatened to unlock the cage where crucial secrets had long been held captive.

THE TWILIGHT MAN
Frank Gruber

Jim Rand lives alone in the California desert awaiting death. Into his hermit existence comes a teenage girl who blows both his past and his brief future wide open.

DOG IN THE DARK
Gerald Hammond

Jim Cunningham breeds and trains gun dogs, and his antagonism towards the devotees of show spaniels earns him many enemies. So when one of them is found murdered, the police are on his doorstep within hours.

THE RED KNIGHT
Geoffrey Moxon

When he finds himself a pawn on the chessboard of international espionage with his family in constant danger, Guy Trent becomes embroiled in moves and countermoves which may mean life or death for Western scientists.

TIGER TIGER
Frank Ryan

A young man involved in drugs is found murdered. This is the first event which will draw Detective Inspector Sandy Woodings into a whirlpool of murder and deceit.

CAROLINE MINUSCULE
Andrew Taylor

Caroline Minuscule, a medieval script, is the first clue to the whereabouts of a cache of diamonds. The search becomes a deadly kind of fairy story in which several murders have an other-worldly quality.

LONG CHAIN OF DEATH
Sarah Wolf

During the Second World War four American teenagers from the same town join the Army together. Forty-two years later, the son of one of the soldiers realises that someone is systematically wiping out the families of the four men.

THE LISTERDALE MYSTERY
Agatha Christie

Twelve short stories ranging from the light-hearted to the macabre, diverse mysteries ingeniously and plausibly contrived and convincingly unravelled.

TO BE LOVED
Lynne Collins

Andrew married the woman he had always loved despite the knowledge that Sarah married him for reasons of her own. So much heartache could have been avoided if only he had known how vital it was to be loved.

ACCUSED NURSE
Jane Converse

Paula found herself accused of a crime which could cost her her job, her nurse's reputation, and even the man she loved, unless the truth came to light.

A GREAT DELIVERANCE
Elizabeth George

Into the web of old houses and secrets of Keldale Valley comes Scotland Yard Inspector Thomas Lynley and his assistant to solve a particularly savage murder.

'E' IS FOR EVIDENCE
Sue Grafton

Kinsey Millhone was bogged down on a warehouse fire claim. It came as something of a shock when she was accused of being on the take. She'd been set up. Now she had a new client — herself.

A FAMILY OUTING IN AFRICA
Charles Hampton and Janie Hampton

A tale of a young family's journey through Central Africa by bus, train, river boat, lorry, wooden bicycle and foot.

THE PLEASURES OF AGE
Robert Morley

The author, British stage and screen star, now eighty, is enjoying the pleasures of age. He has drawn on his experiences to write this witty, entertaining and informative book.

THE VINEGAR SEED
Maureen Peters

The first book in a trilogy which follows the exploits of two sisters who leave Ireland in 1861 to seek their fortune in England.

A VERY PAROCHIAL MURDER
John Wainwright

A mugging in the genteel seaside town turned to murder when the victim died. Then the body of a young tearaway is washed ashore and Detective Inspector Lyle is determined that a second killing will not go unpunished.

DEATH ON A HOT SUMMER NIGHT
Anne Infante

Micky Douglas is either accident-prone or someone is trying to kill him. He finds himself caught in a desperate race to save his ex-wife and others from a ruthless gang.

HOLD DOWN A SHADOW
Geoffrey Jenkins

Maluti Rider, with the help of four of the world's most wanted men, is determined to destroy the Katse Dam and release a killer flood.

THAT NICE MISS SMITH
Nigel Morland

A reconstruction and reassessment of the trial in 1857 of Madeleine Smith, who was acquitted by a verdict of Not Proven of poisoning her lover, Emile L'Angelier.

SEASONS OF MY LIFE
Hannah Hauxwell
and Barry Cockcroft

The story of Hannah Hauxwell's struggle to survive on a desolate farm in the Yorkshire Dales with little money, no electricity and no running water.

TAKING OVER
Shirley Lowe and Angela Ince

A witty insight into what happens when women take over in the boardroom and their husbands take over chores, children and chickenpox.

AFTER MIDNIGHT STORIES,
The Fourth Book Of

A collection of sixteen of the best of today's ghost stories, all different in style and approach but all combining to give the reader that special midnight shiver.